SPADES AND HEARTS

When Sara takes over her aunt's market garden in a small country village, she becomes a part of village life and loses her heart to James, a customer. James initially doubts her capabilities, but finds he's not just interested in the vegetables from her garden . . . Meanwhile, there is Ken, an old rival of James, and there's also Pamela, James' attractive assistant who wants to be more. Love grows and flourishes. Who will harvest, and who'll be left empty-handed?

Books by Wendy Kremer
in the Linford Romance Library:

REAP THE WHIRLWIND
AT THE END OF THE RAINBOW
WHERE THE BLUEBELLS GROW WILD
WHEN WORDS GET IN THE WAY
COTTAGE IN THE COUNTRY
WAITING FOR A STAR TO FALL
SWINGS AND ROUNDABOUTS
KNAVE OF DIAMONDS

WENDY KREMER

SPADES AND HEARTS

Complete and Unabridged

LINFORD
Leicester

First published in Great Britain in 2010

First Linford Edition
published 2011

British Library CIP Data

Kremer, Wendy.
Spades and hearts. - -
(Linford romance library)
1. Love stories.
2. Large type books.
I. Title II. Series
823.9′2–dc22

ISBN 978–1–4448–0740–0

Published by
F. A. Thorpe (Publishing)
Anstey, Leicestershire

Set by Words & Graphics Ltd.
Anstey, Leicestershire
Printed and bound in Great Britain by
T. J. International Ltd., Padstow, Cornwall

This book is printed on acid-free paper

1

'You don't know the first thing about it, do you?' Sara stared at James Conrad and tried to look unconcerned.

'No, but I don't need to! Our gardeners handle planting, growing and harvesting. I'm just responsible for organising the sales, for the deliveries, and running the office.'

His dark eyebrows lifted, and the expression on his well-formed features was slightly haughty, almost arrogant; it showed quite clearly how sceptical he was. In a dubious, but otherwise pleasant tone of voice, he said. 'I imagine it'll be very difficult for you to organize anything if you don't understand basic things like when vegetables are planted, and when they're ready to be harvested. A small business like this depends on providing customers with what they want, and when they want it!'

The girl at his side nodded in silent agreement. She was tall, good-looking with masses of rather beautiful blonde hair and pale grey eyes. She didn't look like the over-worked assistant you'd normally find in a small company — but then the man wasn't run-of-the mill either. Sara studied the woman's face and her figure, and automatically compared her to a pencil — straight lines and no messing about. At least she was allowed to think independently and give her own opinion, because she did so.

'There's much more to managing a well-run office than typing the occasional letter.'

Sara pushed her hands into the pockets of her classically-cut navy trousers; her own hips were more rounded, but she had no problem with that. Mustering her self-control, something she'd learned the hard way after working for various inept and irritating bosses, she replied.

'I do know how to run an office; it

isn't the first time I've been in charge.'

'Oh, you've run a market-garden before, have you?' Pamela Baker asked rather smugly.

Sara's colour heightened and she met the other woman's look directly. It would be stupid to be nettled by someone like her — someone who didn't actually have a final say in the matter.

'No, not a market garden, but I've managed several other businesses for various lengths of time. Office work is office work. Each end product demands a different approach and has varying priorities, but once you know what it's all about, anyone can cope if they are prepared to put in some hard work — and I am.'

With a snooty expression and cut-glass accent, Pamela retaliated.

'That's a wild exaggeration, if I may say so. A well-organised office needs expertise; and that takes a lot of time and skill.'

Sara longed to tell her to take a

running jump, but she reminded herself that her aunt relied on the market garden for a living, and she'd promised to keep it afloat until Aunt Margaret returned. It depended on people like this man and his assistant. She cleared her throat, forced herself to ignore the woman, and concentrated on him. His steely blue eyes examined her closely as she ploughed on. To Sara he looked like a typical successful, no-holds-barred executive; her trained eye left her in no doubt. It wasn't just the quality of his clothes; it was the alert eyes, bland expression and determined chin. They signalled that he knew what he wanted, and how to get it. His bearing also clearly displayed confidence and authority. She realized she'd need to come to terms with him in a way he'd accept; guessing as to what this would be, she decided that he wouldn't want unnecessary frills, impossible promises, or any pussy-footing around on her part.

'I appreciate why you may have

doubts, Mr Conrad, but my aunt had to leave at short notice, because of a family crisis. She took me through everything before she left and I've also plenty of additional instructions and hints. I'm certain I can manage, and I'll make sure you continue to be satisfied with the quality and delivery times. Bill and the other workers are the backbone of the company — they're the ones who produce the vegetables, and that hasn't changed at all. I'm sure the quality will still be first-class, and I'll make sure the rest functions as before. I'm positive we can continue to satisfy your demands.' She paused for a moment; her throat was dry. She had a feeling she hadn't yet completely convinced him.

Making sure she understood why he was there, he continued briskly.

'My company needs unvarying, superior quality. We supply top restaurants in London and elsewhere. I can't afford a hitch of any kind. I need the best, and I need it on time! If I lose a customer, it could have a domino effect. Word gets around fast in my business.'

Sara nodded. She crossed her fingers, hidden in her pocket, assuring him.

'I understand that perfectly. You'll get the top quality, Mr Conrad, and you'll get it on time.'

He stood up, coming to his feet in one quick effortless movement. His assistant hurried to join him. He was very tall, and his long-limbed figure dominated the small office. His dark, curling hair was cut short and tapered to the collar of his pristine shirt. He picked up his shiny leather briefcase and held out his hand.

'If I'm not satisfied, or you don't maintain the terms of our contract, I won't hesitate to look elsewhere for a new supplier. You realise that?'

Sara took his hand; it was large with long fingers, neat nails. It felt warm and not unpleasant. She shook it and met his glance straight on. With more visible boldness than she actually felt, she spoke.

'We'll meet your requirements, on

the dot, as before.'

With a curt nod, he turned on his heel and headed for the door. His movements were economical; they indicated that he was a man who had things under control. Pamela, who looked even more like a pencil walking than when she was sitting down, gave her a knowing look and a curt nod, and followed her boss. Sara wondered briefly how much rigid dieting, and how many visits a week to the fitness studio, had produced that kind of model-like silhouette. Perhaps she was doing her an injustice, but Sara had a distinct feeling Pamela was hoping things would go wrong. She looked like the kind of assistant who wanted to shine, and would welcome anyone else's failure if it heightened her own image in her boss's eyes. Sara couldn't count on much supportive understanding from her.

The small office was a converted outhouse, directly attached to Aunt Margaret's cottage. Behind and around the cottage was the small market garden specialising in organic vegetables. It covered a large area, reaching as far as the fence separating it from the neighbouring farm in the distance. Sara stood back at the sash window after they left, her arms crossed. She watched as his large expensive BMW purred its way down the driveway, swirling up the dried winter leaves as it went. When it reached the open crossbar gate, the silver limousine paused to make sure the road was clear before it sped off down the empty road. Sara sighed and wondered if she had perhaps bitten off more than she could chew. Her present employer had a gap in customer assignments, so he and Sara had agreed it was a perfect moment to use up her overtime, and most of last year's holiday, and laze around for a couple of weeks. She'd been about to book a holiday in sunnier climes, when a phone call from her aunt had radically changed all her plans.

Uncle Bob had died suddenly from a

heart attack two years ago, and although Aunt Margaret wavered, she'd carried on, because a lot of local workers were dependent on the small market garden for a living. Bill, the head gardener, had always been a pillar of strength, and the garden continued to flourish.

Her cousin Gaynor had married a Canadian dentist and moved to Vancouver four years ago. Greg and Gaynor already had one little boy, and Gaynor was now pregnant with twins. Recently complications had set in and Gaynor asked if there was some way her mother could come; she had to be extremely careful and rest as much as possible during the last couple of weeks as there was a danger she could lose the babies. When Sara mentioned casually that her boss had agreed to give her 6-8 weeks off, Aunt Margaret grabbed the chance with both hands. Sara could run the market garden for her, and she'd be free to help Gaynor in Vancouver.

She'd brushed Sara's misgivings aside.

'You've been taking over strange offices at the drop of a hat for years! That's your job. The office work for this place is very simple. I'd be so grateful! So would Gaynor and Greg! Bill handles the practical side of things already, and I'm always there at the end of the phone, or via email. You only have to keep the administrative side of things functioning.'

Sara didn't see how she could refuse, even though the previous businesses she'd been employed to help out temporarily had been industrial or commercial concerns — and mostly based in towns. Sometimes they were within travelling distance of her small flat, but generally not. A market garden in a quiet country area was a completely new challenge.

They'd sent a round-robin letter to all of Aunt Margaret's regular customers explaining about the temporary change in the situation. Several phoned back, some didn't react at all, and only a handful went to the bother to call personally. James Conrad was one of them, and he'd come after her aunt departed, two days ago.

She sighed and ran her neat, pink-tipped fingers through her shiny, dark copper hair. Turning back to the documents spread across the desk, she shuffled through the papers impatiently and switched on the computer. She was trying to figure out exactly what customers had ordered this time last year. After she'd checked whether the same things were available this year, she'd be able to talk to customers with confidence if they put in an order. Aunt Margaret knew by just wandering up and down the trenches what was ready for harvesting; Sara, with little or no experience, had to ask Bill.

She reached the name James Conrad on the customer list, and her thoughts winged back to their interview. Sara was surprised how clearly she could still picture him. She got up and opened one of the small casement windows. It swung out and she rested her hands on the wide windowsill. Her attractive face with its smooth skin, brown eyes framed by long dark lashes, and generous mouth, looked across the neat lines of the garden. The cold, end-of-February winds blew in her face. She could see Bill and another man busily working halfway down one of the long rows.

Her thoughts returned to James Conrad in his navy business suit and camel-hair overcoat — he was an attractive man to look at, and she recalled his deep voice and serious expression. She guessed he was in his early thirties, but his manner made him seem older. Those eyes missed nothing and she felt instinctively that he was someone you wouldn't voluntarily choose as an opponent. Was he married? Perhaps he was bonded with Miss Blondie, or even promised to someone else?

These days, Sara was sceptical about

finding someone to love. She had believed she was in love a couple of times, but she'd been wrong, and now she didn't trust her own judgement any more. Her boyfriends turned out to be less than interested in a long-term relationship, and she'd been constantly disappointed. You couldn't make love happen; and there was no point in pretending that you could. She still hoped she'd be lucky enough to find someone special, but decided even if she never found Mr Right, life could still be rewarding. She was independent, enjoyed her work, and had some good friends and a loving family. She closed the window firmly and fixed the latch. She wondered why her thoughts were circling about love, and not concentrating on the challenge of this new job.

* * *

Sara looked at Bill Withers' weathered face, with lines deeply furrowed from the sun and the wind. He was solid, with thick-muscled arms, a broad chest, and long legs. His baggy trousers were stuffed into the top of his green wellingtons and a padded green waistcoat covered a multi-coloured flannel shirt with sleeves rolled up to his elbows. Sara was wearing a warm anorak and she was in awe that he worked unaware of the cold winds. It was a fine day with patches of sunshine between moments when grey clouds scudded across the sky. The sound of some plucky birds in nearby hedges, and the wind stirring the branches of the trees, heralded the coming of spring, but the stiff breezes blowing at her back were hostile and cold. She listened to him and scribbled quickly on a notepad.

'Thanks! This list will help me to at least *sound* as if I know what I'm talking about. I'll be able to offer the right things when customers make enquiries, or want to place an order.' She brushed the hair out of her face and looked around. 'You're always busy, but you seem to be very busy at the moment; even I can tell that.'

The man's eyes skimmed the garden — his kingdom — and he nodded.

'With spring just round the corner it's a busy time for us. The market garden needs a continuous choice of vegetables, and a big variety. If you don't keep in tune with what customers want, you won't make money.'

'James Conrad called this morning,' Sara said casually. 'I think it was mostly to check me over. He seems to be a very cautious character. He more or less told me that if we don't meet his demands, he'll go elsewhere!'

Bill gave a gruff laugh. 'That's James to a T. Don't worry; he's not quite as daunting as he seems. He's a clever businessman and undoubtedly means what he says. He probably wonders if everything will go haywire without Margaret, but we'll show him, won't we?' He offered her a reassuring smile.

'You know him?' Her curiosity was roused.

'Yes, everyone knows James. He went to the village school with Martin, one of my sons. His parents live in the big red-bricked Victorian house at the end of the village. He makes a good living these days out of supplying top-notch hotels and restaurants. He has his own house not far from here, and Martin tells us he has a holiday home in Brittany.'

'Sounds like he's making money without much personal effort, doesn't it? And he's still comparatively young.'

Bill scratched the back of his head. 'I suppose it does look like that, but I don't think it's quite that straightforward. He has to travel around a lot, looking for sources of good-quality organic food; he deals in meat as well as fruits and vegetables. Meeting the requirements of top-class restaurants is hard work these days. Competition for a good, reliable supplier is still very fierce. If he can't satisfy his customer's expectations, or makes impossible promises, he'd be in dead trouble in no time at all.'

'Well,' Sara squared her shoulders, 'I'll do my best to keep him as a customer. If he's successful as he seems to be, I'll be able to drop his name into the conversation when new customers are fishing for information about 'Wilson's Witchery'. It might just tip the scales in our favour!'

2

A few days later, Sara was flummoxed when she dialled James Conrad's office number and he picked up the phone. Sara was glad he couldn't see her heightened colour. For some reason, she'd expected that Pamela would always be there to sift out, and prevent, any unwanted callers.

'Oh, hello! Sara Benson speaking. About your order, I just wanted to confirm that Tony will bring it round about six; is that okay?'

His deep voice sounded polite and quite pleasant.

'Fine! Once I've checked it, I'll send it straight off to its final destination. It'll reach the restaurants first thing tomorrow morning.'

Sara didn't miss the 'Once I've checked it', but she was confident that they'd meet his standards. The vegetables were in the sorting shed now, being bunched and packed.

There was a slight pause.

'How are you managing?' he asked, to her surprise.

Sara wondered if he was genuinely interested, or just worried in case she wasn't coping.

'Fine, thanks. No problems so far. Everyone is very supportive and I'm gradually finding my feet and enjoying the work.'

'Good, I'll be in touch! And thanks for the information.'

'You're welcome, goodbye!' She heard the click of the phone.

* * *

Sara sorted out the rest of the waiting orders and hung the list on a hook in the sorting shed; Bill checked regularly there from time to time to see what he needed to bring in from the trenches. Once that was finished, she decided to go to the nearby village to do some shopping. As she drove along the country road to the nearby village, she decided spring was definitely in the air. Local farmers were busily turning the rich soil and preparing it for spring planting. It was still cold when the sun vanished, but its rays were gaining strength daily and there was a promise of better things to come.

An old-fashioned bell tinkled as she opened the door. Sara saw it was a delightful village shop. The only alternative would be a large supermarket a few miles away, and anyone without a car would have to depend on the irregular public transport to get them there and back.

There were two women standing near the wooden counter, gossiping They all looked up when she came in and Sara smiled at them quickly before she picked up a wire basket and disappeared between the tightly packed shelves. In one corner was a revolving stand with paperbacks, and a small selection of newspapers and magazines.

She couldn't find her favourite brand of chocolate, but perhaps that was just as well; she was pleased to find almost everything else she needed. She had two overflowing baskets when she reached the counter. One of the women had already left, the other was still chatting to the shop owner. Behind the counter, a friendly woman wearing a wrap-around print pinafore with neat brown hair and rounded pink cheeks smiled at her.

'Did you find all you were looking for, my dear?'

The other woman made room for Sara to put the baskets on the counter.

'Yes, thank you. Is there a butcher's shop in the village?'

The woman started to punch the prices into the old-fashioned cash register.

'Yes, just turn left at the corner. Halfway along the street you'll find Bob Mason, our butcher, next to Dando the newsagents, and there's a baker's shop on the end corner. There aren't any other shops in the village anymore.

There used to be a draper's, a cobbler's, and a sweet shop, but they closed because of the competition from the shops in Hockingdale.' Curiosity finally got the better of her. Without looking up, she asked. 'New to the village, are you? Or just visiting someone? We don't see many strangers here.'

'I'm standing-in for my aunt, Mrs Wilson, until she gets back.'

The woman looked up and smiled broadly.

'Oh, for Maggie? She told me her niece was coming down to help out. So *you're* the clever young lady who takes over the chaos of other people's offices, and sorts them out again?'

'Well, I try.' Sara smiled back at her. 'The market garden is a new kind of challenge, but Bill and the others are an enormous help, otherwise I'd be lost.' She began to pack the goods away into plastic bags.

'Everyone around here knows Maggie,' the shop owner continued. 'We were all shocked when your uncle died so suddenly like that. We admired the way your aunt decided to keep the business running, didn't we Annie?'

The second woman smiled in Sara's direction.

'Yes, she coped wonderfully.' She held out her hand. 'Pleased to meet you, my dear! Welcome to the village! I'm Annie Conrad. I live at the other end of the village, practically the last house.'

Sara studied the woman more carefully; she was James Conrad's mother — Bill said his parents lived in the village. She was fairly tall, had good skin, and light blue eyes. Her dark hair was peppered with grey and pulled back into an elegant small bunch, fixed with a small black velvet bow at the back of her head. Wisps escaping on the sides lessened the severity. She looked high-class; she was a smart woman with good looks and a pleasant expression. Sara took the outstretched hand.

'Thank you! I think I've met your son — James?'

The woman's eyes brightened.

'Oh, yes, of course. He buys from Maggie, doesn't he? I think he has a multitude of sources these days, and his circle of customers has grown a lot faster than even he expected, but Maggie was one of his first suppliers. He's known her all his life.'

Sara nodded. Something her aunt told her came to mind. She looked at Martha, the shop owner. 'My aunt told me she sometimes supplies the shop? Do you still want any surpluses?'

'Yes, anytime — we'll be glad to take them. People are very partial to organic stuff these days, especially when it's local. Maggie and I had an agreement; we split the profit three-ways — the church fund, Maggie and me.'

Sara thought it a quaint arrangement, but reasoned that in a small village commercial rules probably went by the board. Clearly, it was a close-knit community where everyone knew everyone and everything; otherwise, Martha wouldn't have aired the arrangement.

'What a good idea!' Sara smiled warmly. 'And what's the church fund for?'

'Restoring the bell tower; we've been at it for years already. Have you ever visited the church?'

Sara shook her head. She'd never been a regular churchgoer.

'When my parents and I visited Aunt Margaret, it was usually just for the day. We never had a special reason to visit the church, although you can see the tower from the main road. Where is it exactly?'

'You just go round the corner, and straight down the narrow lane opposite,' Mrs Conrad answered. 'Parts of it are nearly a thousand years old. Don't ask me which bits, I don't know, but it is very picturesque. Like a lot of old buildings, though, it needs restoring and rebuilding. At the moment, the bell-tower needs to be strengthened, and it's a specialist job if you don't want to cause historical damage. That's an expensive undertaking, very expensive, but we'll get there one day — everyone is quite determined! There's a bazaar at the church hall this Sunday, after the church service, between twelve and four. The hall is just next to the church. Why don't you come along and see if there's something you fancy — there are the usual things on sale, home-made cakes and jams, things people have donated, a bit of jumble and second-hand books. It'd be a chance for you to meet other people if you're staying in the village for a while.'

'Perhaps I will, if the weather isn't too bad . . . ' Sara said as she finished packing. 'Well, I'm off to the butcher's and then I'll check if any more orders have come in before we finish for the weekend.'

The two women smiled as Sara lifted her hand. The bell tinkled again and she went back to the car with a supply of groceries to last her for a while, and a pretty satisfied feeling.

* * *

She cycled to the village hall; some exercise would do her good. It was a pleasant morning, even though busy clouds were hurrying across a grey sky slashed with occasional ribbons of weak silver sunshine. Aunt Margaret's old cycle went smoothly and she was soon bowling along the empty road at a fast pace. The wind blew in her face and loose strands of hair flowed out from under her red cap like a stream of darkened copper. Her face soon felt cold, but she comforted herself with the thought that the wind would be at her back on the way home. She reached the village a few minutes later, and pedalled on down the lane in the direction of the church. Passing the graveyard and weathered headstones nestling among a group of ancient yew trees, she soon discovered the red-bricked church hall next door to the church. Some people were standing and gossiping outside in the porch-way. She stood her bike against a tree, smiling as she passed them and went inside.

The hall had painted cream walls. The windows had diamond-shaped panes and were set high up. Along one wall there were tidy stacks of wooden chairs. At the end of the long room, there was a curtained stage on a raised rostrum. Some shallow, well-worn wooden steps led up to the stage. The curtain's red velvet material and gold fringes had seen better days and the floor's patterned linoleum had a shabby, cracked appearance and its colours were worn away in some places. A row of trestle tables with the various things on offer were ranged along the empty wall, and continued straight across the hall in front of the stage.

Sara started to wander and examine what was on offer. People who knew each other chattered and the stall-keepers gathered in clusters to talk if no one was showing interest in their wares. On the whole, the room was quiet and fairly empty — there seemed to be more helpers than visitors — but it was still early. Sara extracted her purse and bought a couple of pots of homemade jam and some pickles. There were lots of tables with donated items like knitted scarves, embroidered tablecloths, and cushion-covers. She ambled on, not knowing anyone, but enjoying the countrified, relaxed atmosphere. She reached a table piled high with second-hand books. The trestle-table displayed a good mixture of romance, thrillers, books on gardening, cookery, interior decoration, and some others on history and languages. Near the back, a thick black dictionary with gold lettering in excellent condition waited patiently for a new owner, and right in front were a well-read pile of children's books, and annuals. Busy in the process of looking for something to add to her bedside hoard, she spotted a book by George Matthews. She'd read other books by him; he had an easy style. She was surprised to discover from the blurb on one cover that he'd lived locally, and had even written some of his books in the neighbourhood. His success had carried him to California and a sunnier clime. She turned the book over and jumped when a voice floated over her shoulder.

'That's quite good. I read it not long ago.'

She looked up and the colour rushed to her face when she found James Conrad standing next to her. His blue eyes studied the world with the carelessness of someone with a sharp and somewhat educated mind.

'Hello, Mr Conrad. Did you? I was thinking about buying it. I read *Alone At Dawn* recently and a couple of others, but I can't remember all the titles. He's a good writer.'

He nodded in agreement.

'Yes, he is, isn't he? That's just as

good. It's a bit brutal in parts, but I suppose it has to be, to make the story exciting enough. And, please, I'm James. I know that your name is Sara — from the signature on your bill.'

She nodded. She looked down at the book to give herself time to sort out her reaction. She handed over the money for three books she'd chosen to the man behind the table. Surprised to see someone like him in a village bazaar, she spoke.

'I've bought these books and some jam. What have you bought?'

He glanced around and lowered his voice. There was an upward turn to his mouth and his eyes sparkled briefly. Sara thought how the fleeting expression changed him. He lifted a plastic bag.

'To tell the truth, I've bought some atrocious looking mugs, a couple of CDs by people I've never heard of, and some cake from my mother's stall!'

She looked surprised. Reassured by the relaxed expression on his face, Sara felt free to ask his motives.

'Why did you buy them if you don't like them, or don't want them?'

'Oh, I'm keen on the cake, but as far as the rest is concerned, I bought them without a purpose, just simply because I daren't leave without buying a couple of things! When one of these bell-tower collecting efforts takes place, and my mother knows that I'm not away on business, she expects me to turn up and empty my wallet!'

Sara felt something inside her wobble as she saw how the serious businessman softened and became a perfectly normal human being — at least for now.

'So, in other words, you've given in to blackmail?'

The corners of his mouth turned up and he smiled softly.

'Oh, I wouldn't call it blackmail. I'd define it as manipulative pressure! She's my mother!'

'I'm surprised you let her get away with it. I'd have thought you'd fight anyone who was trying to manipulate you, in any way.'

'Really?' His eyebrows lifted. 'Probably that's true, but in this case resistance is futile — you haven't met my mother!'

Sara shoved the books into the plastic bag to join the jam and pickles.

'Wrong! I met her in the shop. She seems to be a very nice person.'

He shoved his hands into the pocket of his Barbour coat and eyed her speculatively.

'Did you? Oh, I agree, she is nice, but under that polite exterior is a will of iron, and now that she's also a fully-fledged member of the bell-tower funding committee, it means 'full steam ahead' until that heap of stones has a suitable steel corset at last!'

Sara was tempted to say he'd clearly inherited his mother's determination, but she didn't.

'Why don't you just give her a donation? A lump sum; then you wouldn't be forced to show your face all the time?'

'I can assure you there's no point; I've already tried that. She insists on team spirit, and expects me to be loyal to the village of my birth. My father would also prefer to potter around his garden today, but she's installed him behind the fresh fruit stall over there instead.' He tilted his head to the side.

She bit her lip lightly, trying not to laugh.

'What on earth do you do with the things you've bought, if you don't want to keep them? Do you throw them in the bin?'

He caught her arm lightly, turned her away from the tables, and lowered his voice again like a secret agent revealing state secrets.

'Ah! That's another sore point. I have a couple of boxes full of the stuff in the garage. I'm planning to offer them back for resale sometime or other.'

She tried to look serious.

'I think you highly under-estimate people's memories. The people who donated them will spot them straight off and feel insulted.'

'Think so? Perhaps I ought to dump them in a charity shop a fair distance from here?'

She nodded enthusiastically.

'A much better idea I would think! Not so much danger involved there!' She paused. 'Why don't you just dump them in your rubbish bin?'

He studied her and smiled briefly, his blue eyes twinkling. Sara had found it hard to compare him to the serious, no-nonsense, businessman who'd sat opposite her in the office the other day.

'Ah! Anyone can tell you're new to the village! The men who empty the bins are highly-trained informers! Now and then, they check — officially, they are entitled to do so — in case someone uses the bin to get rid of unauthorized rubbish. They are also better organized than the KGB, and I'm quite sure that if they noticed that I was throwing perfectly useful items away, the information would eventually seep back to my mother. I'd really be in the frying pan then, and have to live with lectures about throwing away perfectly useful items for several weeks.'

'Yes.' She smiled broadly. 'If it's like that, you face a real problem. Transport them somewhere else — that's the only way out!'

He nodded and his smile showed dazzlingly white, even teeth.

They were suddenly interrupted by his mother and they looked at each other secretly. 'James! You came after all!' Mrs Conrad looked at him approvingly. 'Do you know Sara? We met in the shop the other day.'

'So I'm told.' He looked at her indulgently and Sara sensed that no matter what he said, these two people liked each other. 'And before you ask — yes, I have bought something!'

Mrs Conrad straightened the cardigan of her jonquil coloured twin-set and centred her pearl necklace with its jewelled clasp.

'Good! I'll see you later on then? Don't forget to visit your dad's stall and buy some of his apples. Everyone eats apples, even you. And don't ask if they are a bio-product, just buy some!'

'Okay!' He laughed.

After giving Sara a farewell smile, Mrs Conrad hurried off back to her stall where someone was studying the collection of cakes she had on offer.

'See what I mean?' He looked at Sara and creased his forehead.

Sara laughed.

'She's obviously enjoying herself, and she's working for a good cause. Would you prefer her to sit in a corner, knitting and waiting for you to call?'

'James! Fancy seeing you here!'

A young man sidled up to them from a group of people who'd just crossed the threshold. He had blond hair that reached the collar of his shirt in the back and flopped over his forehead in the front. His jovial greenish eyes viewed them with a speculative glance. His clothes were casual, loose and well-worn; comfortable brown corduroy pants, a pale sweater over a flannel shirt open at the neck, and loafers on his feet.

Sara noticed a change in James Conrad's expression. He stiffened and the shutters came down again.

'Ken! It's not really your scene either, is it?'

'No! I'm here for the same reason as you, I expect. My mother played on the theme of 'duty to the village of my birth'.' He nodded downwards with his chin towards some books piled under one arm. He handed them to the chap behind the counter with a nod. 'I promised to sort some out for the book stall.' He smiled easily and his glance wandered to Sara. 'Who's this then, your latest girlfriend? You know that it's absolutely fatal to bring a girl within two miles of this place without being labelled as engaged, married and settled down.' He waited for an answer.

Sara coloured, although she knew it was a completely stupid reaction.

With an edge of stiffness to his voice, James replied.

'This is Sara Benson; she's helping out at the market garden while Maggie's away. Sara, meet Ken Fellows.'

Ken ran his fingers through the hair that fell untidily across his brow. His eyes lit up, and he grinned.

'Oh, yes, my mother mentioned you. Good! A fresh face in the place at last! And a good-looking one, too! What do you think of the village, Sara?'

Her eyes sparkled.

'Do you honestly expect me to say something negative? I'm new here, and I must admit I'm still finding my feet. I gather that you come from the village?'

'Yep! Now you're here, I'm sorry I've left. I have a bookshop in Hockingdale. I wouldn't mind having one here — I rather like the place, even if it *is* centuries behind the times — but at the moment it wouldn't pay. There aren't enough customers to make it a viable prospect.'

'I can imagine,' Sara replied. 'It's not even directly on the main road . . . '

'I haven't completely buried the idea. I'm trying to build up a good number of regular customers, so that they'll follow me if I move back, and I'm also looking into internet sales, to fill the gaps on any day-to-day sales.'

'You'd need premises, wouldn't you?' Practical thoughts made her ask.

'That's one advantage of the place. Hockingdale is more expensive; I could get something much cheaper here. You know the village shop?'

She nodded.

'That's my Mum and Dad's. There are a couple of empty shops round the corner from them. With a bit of capital and a bank loan, it might work.'

James Conrad added his unasked for opinion.

'Unless you want to go under fast, you need plenty of opening capital to get you through the initial period; until you're really established.'

'Oh, James!' Ken made a wry face. 'Sometimes you have to take risks; lay your destiny in the lap of the gods and see what happens!'

James's lips were a thin line. He shrugged.

'I don't believe in throwing money down the drain. You have to work hard to earn money; risks should be calculable.' He paused. 'Anyway, it's none of my business what you do, is it?' He looked around. 'Better pay my father a visit.' He managed a faint parting smile for Sara. ''Bye!' He turned away, to stride determinedly towards the other side of the hall. Sara decided something was off beam between the men; there was a tense feeling.

Ken dropped his arm casually round her shoulder. Sara didn't welcome the familiarity but didn't want to fuss.

'So, Sara, you're here to support the bell tower fund? Have you seen it?'

'The bell tower? No.'

'Thought so.' He laughed. 'Come on, I'll take you around the church and show you the damage, then we'll come back here and have a cup of tea.'

Sara felt overruled by his manner, but it would be silly to refuse. His offer was quite innocent, and she was quite capable of abandoning him if necessary. With his arm still draped around her shoulder, he propelled them towards the door. Out of the corner of her eye, she saw James talking to someone. He gazed speculatively at them as they were leaving.

3

After a couple of minutes with Ken, she could tell he was a very colourful and gregarious character. She wondered if something unpleasant had happened between him and James, but she didn't ask. James was serious and introverted; a complex character who didn't reveal the intimate side of his nature to a mere stranger. Ken treated life lightly; he was buoyant, open and bright and breezy. His attitude could lead to friction and misunderstandings when the chips were down because his characteristics didn't always go hand in hand with reliability.

Just before Ken had dragged her away, she'd spotted a real spark of humour beneath the smokescreen of James's mask. That brief insight had impressed her more than any of the present avalanche of convivial wit and camaraderie from Ken. Why did a devil-may-care character who floated through life enjoying everything, attract her less than someone who was remote, withdrawn, and very likely a rather exacting person? It probably came down to a gut-reaction; whether you felt comfortable with, or rejected, specific qualities.

Sara followed Ken through the church, and listened as he pointed out things of interest. She could tell he was making an effort to pass on interesting information about the old building. He was very well informed, so he wasn't someone with just bubbles in his brain. He liked to laugh and joke and he made her laugh, too. He wasn't so egoistical that he didn't listen to her — but she still felt there was something missing to make him someone she'd like to know a great deal better.

At the end of the tour, they meandered around the tower to appraise the damage, and then headed back towards the church hall. On the way, he spotted someone he knew coming towards them.

'Go ahead! Get yourself some tea; this could take a little time. Mr Wright is manager of the local bank and it's a good chance for me to casually mention my plans and get his initial reaction. I've known him all my life, so he's not likely to shake me off and suggest an appointment at the bank. If I don't see you later on, I hope we'll meet again soon. Pop into the shop when you come into Hockingdale!'

Sara nodded and, after a brief introduction, she left the two men and went into the hall again. She thought about directly cycling home, but then decided a cup of tea would be just the thing to armour her against the return journey. In the church hall, there were now a lot more people milling about, and she headed straight for the corner where two women were busy making coffee and tea, and selling small cakes. Sara met James Conrad coming away with a tea cup in one hand and an iced-slice in the other. When their eyes linked, she could see he was surprised.

'Where's Ken?' he said smoothly, with no expression on his face.

'Trying to ingratiate himself with the local bank manager!'

'And you've come back for tea?' A glint of humour returned.

She nodded.

'I thought about going home, but I decided I needed one of the cakes and a cup of tea to give me energy to cope with the winds instead!'

'That means you're here on a bike; or did you walk?'

'It may not be the best time of year to cycle, but the road is flat all the way and I quite enjoyed it.'

The beginnings of a smile touched the corner of his mouth, and Sara held her breath for a fraction of a second. How ridiculous!

'What would you like? Tea or coffee? I've picked an iced-slice. What do you want?'

'I must admit, I'm a chocolate éclair addict — they had some wonderful ones on offer when I arrived. And I'd like coffee, please.'

'They come from Fred's Bakery, and I'm sure you've never tasted better; they melt in the mouth.'

She hunted in her bag for her purse, but he brushed it aside.

'I'll take this coffee,' she said. 'It might be cold before you come back. I'll grab a table.'

In minutes, he was back with her éclair and another coffee and he then folded his long form into the chair and leaned back. Sara took a bite and the cream oozed out on the sides. She put it down, wiped the corners of her mouth with the tip of her fingers.

'Mmmm! Delicious! I see what you mean about them being good.'

'Like to try?' He picked up his plate and held it out in her direction.

'Thanks very much, but no. I'll buy an iced-slice next time I'm shopping in the village. Enjoy that one yourself'

He did, and studied her. James liked her arresting face, temptingly curved mouth, and mass of lustrous dark bronze hair. She barely reached his shoulder, yet she managed to look regal, tall and trim. He particularly liked her eyes; they were liquid brown with long lashes, and they glowed.

'Do you live in the village?'

He hooked the plain white cup and took a sip.

'No, about five miles away. I'm fond of my parents, but a healthy distance helps to maintain a decent relationship.'

Sara smiled and nodded.

'I know what you mean. I love my mum and dad, but parents are parents. They tell you they've let go, but they still want to know everything, don't they! Did you know Ken is planning an evening of book reading and signing with George Matthews at his shop? I don't know the exact date; I forgot to ask.'

'Is he? No, I didn't! It might be worth a look in.'

'That's what I thought, too.' She smiled. 'I might go.'

'When you know the exact date, let

me know.' As an afterthought, he added, 'Perhaps we could go together?'

The breath caught in her throat, but her voice sounded perfectly calm.

'Yes, that would be nice.' Sara speculated whether he meant it or was just being polite.

He leaned back and looked relaxed as he told her about people in the village and anecdotes about the past. He didn't mention anything about himself and nothing about Ken either. Cups and plates empty, they took their dishes back, parted civilly and went their separate ways again.

Sara was already a fair distance down the road, when his BMW went past. He tooted the horn and he lifted his hand. The bike wobbled slightly as she let go of the handlebar to return his greeting.

* * *

Things at the market garden were running smoothly, thanks to Bill's support, and Aunt Margaret's organised system.

She hadn't yet worked out the exact order of availability of the vegetables in her brain but, with Bill's help, she'd made a chart for the office wall, so that when customers made initial enquiries, she had a vague idea of what would be available and when. The winds were still chilly, and the nights were cold.

Ken sent her a flyer about George Matthews's visit with a handwritten *Hope you'll come* at the bottom of the page. She'd hesitated about sending it on to James, but she recalled their conversation and decided she would. It was up to him if he went or not. She redirected the flyer to his office address with a short note of explanation, and marked it *Personal*. If she secretly hoped for an answer of some kind, she was disappointed.

* * *

Visiting the local market town a few days later to deliver some crates of winter vegetables to a local hotel, she met James Conrad on her way back to the van. He was as well-dressed and formal as the day they met in her office. Her heart skipped a beat. Pamela was walking alongside and he didn't notice her until she gained his whole attention when she said hello.

'Sara! Morning! What are you doing here?'

'Delivering vegetables to the Red Heart.'

'Can't someone else do that?' He asked. 'Crates of veg weigh tons.'

'Oh, I manage. It's a waste of time to take one of the men out of the garden just to lift crates for a couple of minutes.'

Pamela smiled surreptitiously but didn't comment. Sara guessed nothing would induce Pamela to do something as unfeminine as lifting a crate of vegetables. Sarah took her courage in her hands.

'Will I see you this evening?'

His dark brows lifted.

'This evening? I'll be on the motorway this evening. I'm meeting someone in Nantes early tomorrow.'

She was glad she reacted quickly, and showed no surprise.

'Oh, yes! Well, have a safe journey.' She was ready to turn away.

He was puzzled; his hand wavered, lost in mid-air.

'What's happening this evening? Anything important?'

Sara didn't want to hang around, and certainly didn't want to explain, especially with Pamela standing at his side. It wasn't likely he'd have gone anyway. It had taken a lot of willpower to send him her note in the first place, and she certainly wasn't going to push herself forward now. He'd probably thrown the flyer in the wastepaper-bin after a fleeting glance and not deemed it worthy of a reply. She faced the two of them and hoisted her shoulder bag.

'No! Nothing important!' she said, swallowing a tinge of disappointment.

Pamela hurried him along impatiently.

'James, we have to finish off the cost estimate before we leave. If we miss the ferry, we won't get a cabin on a later one; the night crossings are always booked out.' She looking down at her wristwatch with irritation.

James ran his hand through his hair.

Sara noted that Pamela had talked about a 'cabin' not 'cabins'. She gave them a fleeting smile and automatically straightened her shoulders.

'I won't keep you then. 'Bye!' She turned and went on her way.

She drew in a deep breath and walked quickly, not paying attention to where she was going. She bumped into one or two people and apologised before she pulled herself together and wondered why it had mattered so much. She'd go this evening anyway. She'd keep her hairdressing appointment, and she'd wear what she'd chosen with such care.

* * *

She looked around and liked the appearance of Ken's bookshop; it was a place to rummage and poke around in until you found something you fancied. There were comfortable leather chairs in quiet corners and books from floor to ceiling everywhere.

He greeted her like a life-long acquaintance on her arrival, but she was one of dozens of invited people and she made no attempt to monopolise his attention. She helped herself to a glass of wine while waiting for people to arrive for the talk. In the end, the evening turned out to be a partial success. Another woman struck up a conversation about the author, and they were both glad to have found someone to talk to. They were still chatting when George Matthews began his talk. He was interesting and he scattered reminiscences about local places into his talk. She was able to concentrate without distraction. She bought his latest book and afterwards she and her neighbour stood in line to get the book signed. Not long after, a taxi driver called out the name 'Miller!' and her new acquaintance gave her an apologetic look and left quickly. Ken waved at her from across the room; he was in the midst of a crowd of people surrounding George Matthews. She was thinking of leaving — perhaps she'd call on her best friend Sandra on the way home. Still undecided, someone bumped into her — an old customer who immediately laid claims to her. For a couple of minutes she was pleased. Who needed James Conrad; the world was full of other men. Her slight exhilaration was short-lived. Crushed together in a corner, she noticed he'd drunk too much and was talking nonsense. If he carried on drinking the gratis wine on offer at his present rate, she'd end up being responsible for getting him home. She left when he went searching for yet another refill. On the drive back to Aunt Margaret's, she enjoyed the solitude and travelling through the darkness on her own; there was much to be said for being single and independent. She'd phone Sandra on Monday. Perhaps she'd like to come down and stay one weekend . . .

* * *

It had been a busy morning so far and it was still only nine-thirty; the phone hadn't stopped. She ought not to complain, it was good for business.

''Morning, 'Wilson's Witchery'!'

'That's a rather ridiculous name for an organic garden. Where did it come from?'

His voice made her insides jump, but the question gave her time to adjust before she answered.

'Yes, it is, isn't it? My aunt told me there's a rumour that a witch used to live on this spot in the middle-ages, and when they started the business, my aunt hoped any lingering witch-lore would be favourable. You come from here, you should know that.'

'I didn't — or if I ever did, I've forgotten.' He laughed softly. 'I wonder what strangers think when they hear 'Witchery'.'

'They're probably intrigued. I'm sure they don't imagine my aunt brews the vegetables up in a cauldron out in the back shed. It's a very effective book-mark. It sounds a lot more exciting than 'Wilson's Market' or 'Wilson's Organic Products'. I like it!'

'Perhaps the witch in you is emerging?'

'I hope that's meant in the nicest sense of the word? All women are witches in one way or another, aren't they?' He laughed and she went on. 'This is a very senseless conversation, early on a Monday morning. What can I do for you? You need vegetables?'

'No — I'll get back to you about that later on in the day. I wanted to apologise. I didn't realise that George Matthews was in Hockingdale last Friday evening. I didn't find your note until this morning.'

'Oh! I promised I'd let you know about it — at the church sale.'

'Yes, I remember. I'm sorry I missed it. Was it good?'

Her breath quickened.

'Yes. He was entertaining, and gave us some insight into his private motivations for writing and told some anecdotes about his life in general.'

'I have two trays for mail,' James explained. 'One for urgent stuff, and one for less urgent. Your note got mixed up with the less urgent stuff.'

'A note reminding you about a reading in a bookshop is hardly urgent.'

'But it was a personal letter and they always get priority treatment. I don't know why Pamela mixed things and put it in the wrong tray.' Sara could guess why — the woman didn't like her — but she didn't say so, and he continued. 'I was puzzled when you asked about Friday evening; now I understand. You should have explained — perhaps I could have re-organised.'

'It wasn't that important, and I doubt

if you could have cancelled your meeting in France at such short notice.'

'Possibly not, but you must have thought me extremely bad-mannered to ignore your message and pretend I didn't know what you were talking about?'

Unseen by him she shrugged.

'You're busy; these things happen. Don't give it a second thought!'

'Perhaps I can make it up to you one day? An evening out perhaps?'

Sara was lost for words. She tried to lighten the conversation, and in a relaxed tone, she said. 'An evening out, with a potential witch? That would be dangerous!'

'Agreed! A bit of a gamble, and a venture into the unknown, but conceivably Ken was right about taking uncalculated risks sometime. I'll phone later with a list of what I need Wednesday afternoon.'

'Right! Till later, then.'

''Bye!' There was a click and the phone went dead.

Sara was silent for a moment, the phone still in her hand. She was pleased there'd been a plausible reason he'd forgotten, but she vowed she wouldn't make any more stupid mistakes and place too much importance on what James said or did from now on. He hadn't made a definite date, either.

* * *

Sara was delivering a crate to a small restaurant in a nearby village when she noticed James's BMW. Her good intentions of paying no heed went up in smoke, and her heart began to race. For a brief moment, she wished that she was wearing something more attractive than an old anorak, jeans and a pair of purple wellingtons. She lifted the wooden crate out of the boot, locked the car and went to the side entrance. Perhaps he was eating in the restaurant with a guest and she wouldn't see him. She put the box down, opened the door, picked it up again and went inside. James was standing in the centre of the kitchen, talking to the chef. He looked up and a smile touched the corner of his mouth.

'This is a nice surprise! Delivering vegetables? Filching my business?'

She tried to sound offhand and ignore how fast her heart was beating.

'Wilson's Witchery has always supplied this restaurant.' She smiled and was rewarded by a forthcoming and warm expression. 'I'm sure you won't end up in the poorhouse if we sell them some vegetables now and then!'

The chef was a Frenchman and he listened with interest; his gaze wandered back and forth between them. '*À vos marques, prêts, partez!*'

James laughed. Sara was pleased by the way his face had lost its severity and how he suddenly looked younger.

'No, there's not really any competition, Jacques! I've no intention of chasing her round your table; she has an advantage over me in those wellingtons.'

'What are you doing here?' she asked, trying to sound relaxed.

He stuck one hand in the pocket of his loose overcoat; the material was rich in quality and a soft beige colour. It swirled gently about his dark blue business suit.

'I supply Jacques with meat!'

'Oh! What a perfect combination — our vegetables and your meat!'

'Mind boggling, I agree! Tell you what; I invite you to have lunch with me.'

'Here? Now? Me looking like a farm-worker fresh from mucking out?'

He eyed her from top to toe and rubbed his chin.

'I have to use my instinct to pick out quality. You'll pass! Come on!'

Sara couldn't think of anything she'd enjoy more.

'If we can sit in a quiet corner, okay, but not if I'm centre stage.'

He shrugged.

'You look perfectly presentable to me. I'm sure no one else in or around

Hockingdale has such beautiful wellingtons!' He caught her elbow, and with a nod to Jacques who gave him a thumbs-up sign, he guided her out of the kitchen, down a corridor and into the half-empty dining room. He helped her out of her anorak, and she was glad her sweater was fit to be seen. Her black jeans and purple wellingtons would be out of sight, under the table.

He asked for one of the corner tables. Once seated, Sara looked around. The nearby window overlooked the empty terrace. Beyond that, the half-tamed garden meandered down to the willows on the edge of the fast flowing river. Sara decided it would be a delightful place to sit in summer.

At present, she was content to be in the restaurant's low-ceilinged, beamed dining room, opposite the rather attractive James Conrad.

His strong features softened as he saw how the wind had whipped colour into her cheeks. Loose tendrils of her rich, auburn hair framed her quiet oval face with its unblemished skin and inviting lips. He studied her for a moment and admired the lines of her seductive young body and wholesome looks.

Her breath caught in her throat and she felt her heart pounding. Somehow, her voice was coloured in neutral tones when she looked at him.

'This is nice. I haven't been here before — I've only ever got as far as the kitchen when I deliver the vegetables.'

'Then it's about time you did. Would you like to choose, or leave it up to me?' His tone was just as even as hers, with a touch of amusement.

Sara put down the large menu she'd just picked up.

'That's an excellent idea! And as my menu is in French, I'm sure you understand it much better than I do.'

'They've given you one from the wrong pile!' He smiled. 'There are quite a few French families who come here, now and then, because of Jacques. Anything you don't like eating?'

The skin on her nose wrinkled.

'I don't like crab, and I don't like calamari either.'

'But you like fish in general?'

'Yes.' Sara nodded.

He glanced at the menu and looked up again.

'How about *mousse de saumon*, followed by *filet mignon aux oignions avec gratin dauphinois, plateau de fromages et salade verte*, and finishing off with *crème caramel*?'

'My mouth's watering already!'

'I was hoping to impress you with my French, but I can tell I haven't made an impact! Do you know what it all means?'

'I think so. Filet mignon is pork, isn't it? I understand the rest.'

He nodded.

'You speak French?'

'I took French in school, but I've never used it. The closest I ever got was when I was in the sixth form and we went skiing in the French Alps. I only ever needed to use simple sentences, so

I've forgotten everything worthwhile.'

'You seem to understand enough to follow what I'm about to order, so it hasn't completely disappeared.' He caught the eye of a passing waitress and she took their order.

By the time the first course arrived, he was telling her about his holiday home in Brittany. She had to explain first where she'd heard about it.

James nodded.

'Bill's son and I went to school together. Martin doesn't live locally any more, but he was a good pal. I see him sometimes when he visits his parents. I probably mentioned the cottage at some time or another. I wasn't intending on trying to impress anyone, least of all Martin.'

'I don't think Martin thought so either — he just passed the information on. It sounds wonderful.' She sighed softly. 'A cottage by the sea!' He was a handsome man and she was acutely conscious of his athletic stature.

He shrugged and picked up his fork.

'It was a bargain. The grandfather of one of my suppliers lived there until he died. No one wanted to take it over because it had to be split five ways — and no one wanted to keep it and pay the others off. In the end they decided to sell it, and as it would have cost a great deal to modernize it before it could be put up for a decent price, they were quite happy to accept my offer. I took it over lock, stock and barrel. They just took what they wanted to keep. I got rid of most of what they left, but kept one or two pieces of the furniture because I think they'll look really good when I can afford to have them restored properly. I've had the place re-wired, had central heating installed and the drainage renewed. I hope I can do most of the rest myself, whenever I have the time and a bit of ready cash.'

'Sounds like you were lucky!'

'I think I was. I haven't visited it much since I bought it. Last summer I spent a week re-plastering one of the bedrooms, painting it, buying a new bed and generally making at least one room habitable. I'm planning to get all the rooms finished in the same way. Time is the sticking point. If I'm in France these days, it's never for long, and I'm usually in another region and on business. Perhaps I'll manage a couple of weeks there this summer. Someone in the village keeps an eye on it for me. One day, when it's all finished, I'll just sit outside with a glass of red wine and watch the fishermen busy in the small harbour down below and enjoy it.' Munching a forkful of mousse, he went on. 'It's only a small place, two rooms up and down, but it's what life is all about.'

'Then you ought to find more time to enjoy it!'

He ran his hand through his thick hair. It fell back neatly into place.

'I suppose I should, and I'm always intending to make time, but then work gets in the way.'

'Would you like to live there permanently?' Sara's dish was almost empty.

'No. I like England too much for that. My roots, my work, my family, my friends are here — but I love Brittany. It would be ideal to be able to split my time. And I'd like to assimilate more into the community, but I'll have to make a real effort to do that.'

The next course arrived and James asked her about her family and where she lived. The pork was wonderfully tender and the potatoes creamy. Sara tried not to hurry so that she could appreciate the food properly and also so that she could enjoy his company as long as possible.

'I rent a small, two-roomed flat. Sometimes I'm too far away to travel back and forth because of the job — then the company pays for accommodation, usually it's a hotel. I'd love to own my own house, and I'm saving towards that, but there's no point in buying anything unless I know I'll be fixed somewhere on a permanent basis.'

'I gather that you're a kind of trouble shooter?'

She nodded.

'I work for someone who sends us round to sort things out when they go wrong, or I stand in for someone else in an emergency like a long illness.'

'Us? Who are us?'

'There are five of us; qualified in different things. My boss is an accountant, I handle any office problems, Suzy is a qualified bookkeeper, and Clive is our computer whizz-kid.'

'What would you like to do on a permanent basis?'

She laughed softly.

'I don't know. The trouble with helping in an emergency is that you never know what a company is like when it all runs smoothly. It'd be nice to work for a boss I like, doing something interesting and responsible, for longer than a couple of weeks.'

Waving a fork in the air, he commented.

'You're independent and capable. I

bet you could run your own company. If you go on working for someone else, you'll never discover your own potentials. Think about it!'

'I'm not sure I have enough guts to do that.'

'You have nerve enough to go into completely strange companies — running your own company wouldn't be more difficult. You don't need huge overheads to start something like that either. You don't even need your own premises at first; you could run it from home till it takes off. You need to be sure there's a market; the rest is determination and hard work.'

The conversation drifted and wandered. By the time they'd finished the *crème caramel*, they both agreed they wouldn't be able to eat again for a week. They'd moved on to a new level of friendship. Sara didn't want to think of anything beyond now; it was enough for the moment. As she studied his face across the table, she was already sure that he was a type of man she wouldn't forget. She didn't want to analyze why. It was sufficient that she'd had a glimpse of the man behind the business mask.

Their tête-a-tête was interrupted by his cell phone.

'Yes, I haven't forgotten!' He listened. 'No, I've met a friend and we had lunch together. Time just ran away.' His lips thinned slightly. 'Pamela, I don't need your permission to juggle my daily appointments. I haven't missed anything important, I didn't let anyone down, and I'll be back in time for the meeting with Lionel.'

Pamela was clearly trying to smooth out his obvious irritation with some suitable glib explanations, but Sara could see he was still slightly annoyed. She moved her attention to the window and looked out towards the grey river flowing swiftly like a never-ending snake at the end of the lawn and tried to ignore his conversation.

'Right! Till later then.'

She looked at him.

'Our lunching together has caused snags?'

He seemed to relax again and eased into a smile.

'No; not at all. I've thoroughly enjoyed our meal together.'

'Yes, so have I. Thank you!' She looked at her watch. 'Gosh! Look at the time! I told Bill I'd be back in an hour! I bet they're wondering where I am.'

'But at least no one actually knows where you are! Sometimes one shouldn't have any regrets!'

A small smile of enchantment touched her lips as she watched him.

'I'll agree with that wholeheartedly! And I have absolutely no regrets.'

4

Looking out of the office window, Sara noticed a strange car coming up the driveway; it stopped near the office door. She went out, thinking it was a regular customer. The blue Ford parked neatly and, when the door opened, out stepped Mrs Conrad.

Her surprise at seeing James's mother was in Sara's voice.

'Mrs Conrad! What can I do for you?' Sara was still holding the bundle of papers that she'd been working on in the office; they were fighting bravely with the blustery breezes.

'Ah! I'm hoping you can save my life! I have some guests for dinner this evening and I planned to have a very traditional meal of lamb with mint sauce, carrots, peas and cabbage — but Martha has no cabbages. I want to save myself a trip to the supermarket. Can you sell me one?'

Sara laughed softly.

'I think so! Come with me. Bill has harvested half a row this morning. They're in the shed over there, waiting to be tidied up and packed, ready for delivery to one of our customers later this afternoon.'

'Tidy them up?'

Sara led the way, and James's mother fell in at her side. She explained.

'The mud is washed off, any loose leaves are removed, and they're sorted according to size and weight.'

'For a moment, I had a vision of them being brushed and combed and tied up with a decorative yellow bow!'

'Brushing and combing wouldn't improve their appearance much.' Sara laughed. 'But a yellow ribbon would be quite an eye-catcher. I'll have to pass that idea onto Aunt Margaret. A paper band with our name and logo — that's not a bad idea at all!' They reached the long packing shed and Sara opened the door and stood aside to let Mrs Conrad pass. Sara had come out without a coat and was glad to get inside out of the cool winds.

The large shed had sheet metal walls. Daylight fell on a long central table through transparent plastic sheeting in the roof and there was also overhead strip-lighting hanging above the table. Along one wall were some water troughs with pressurized hoses. A couple of low, cage-like, containers were piled high with cabbages and flat cardboard boxes were on the table waiting to be filled. The other wall was full of shelves with folded boxes, pots and packing materials. Sara gestured towards the cabbages. Her voice echoed through the shed when she said, 'Help yourself!'

Mrs Conrad picked out one of the smaller cabbages.

'This is perfect. We're only six people, so this will be plenty.' Holding it in her hands, she continued. 'It's lovely and firm and couldn't be fresher!'

'Anything else?' Sara asked.

'That's all, thanks,' Mrs Conrad replied. 'How much?'

Sara brushed the question aside.

'Please! You're welcome!'

'That's very kind; I'd like to repay you though. Come and have a cup of tea one afternoon when you're in the village!'

'Thanks, perhaps I will.'

'No perhaps! Come next time you go shopping. A quick phone call will tell you we're at home, and then I'll put the kettle on straight away!' She looked at her watch. 'The dessert for this evening takes a couple of hours to set, so I'd better be off. I hope it works, you can never be sure when you try something new!'

* * *

Sara wavered, but finally decided to go. She phoned Mrs Conrad before she started out.

'Lovely! I'm glad you rang. James is

here, I'm sure he'll be glad to see you.'

Sara was so startled she forgot to offer to bring some cake from Fred's. The information that James was visiting his parents made her spontaneous visit more tempting and she felt some elation. She renewed her make-up, changed into a smart pencil skirt and soft caramel sweater and told herself she'd have made the same effort if she'd just been visiting his mother.

The weather was mild, and there were definite patches of green in the hedges as she sped past. After completing her shopping quickly, she drove to the end of the village and parked on the road outside the red-bricked Victorian detached house. The entrance porch had a modern outer door of double-glazing in a Victorian design. Inside, it had the original tiles, and the genuine Victorian door with its panels of patterned glass. She used the brass knocker, and a blurred figure approached down the hallway.

James opened the door, and gave her a friendly smile. She felt a warm glow when he said. 'Hullo, come in!' He stood aside for her to pass and closed the door again. Helping her out of her short jacket, he gave her slender body an appreciating look and studied the golden specks in her brown eyes for a few seconds before he pointed towards the door at the end of a long narrow corridor. 'The sitting room!'

She went, soft footed and moving easily ahead of him.

'I promised to call on your mother next time I was in the village. I didn't expect to see you.'

'Yes, she told me and she also told me she'd got a cabbage off you for nothing — bad business acumen that!' His deep voice was humorous and it bounced along the walls as they went. 'Luckily you phoned when I was here otherwise I'd have missed you. After you phoned, I decided to hang on a bit longer, and have tea with you.'

He'd chosen to wait because she was

coming; Sara didn't understand why, but she felt very pleased. She had a feeling of smug delight as he edged past her and opened the door. He was so close she couldn't remember how to breathe. He made her senses spin and she noted the spicy smell of his aftershave. His mother came towards her.

'I'm glad you came, Sara. I don't think you've met my husband, have you?' She indicated towards a distinguished tall man with grey hair, lively dark eyes and a friendly face. 'Gareth, this is Sara.' He held out his hand.

'Pleased to meet you! My wife and James have a head start on me, but I'll soon catch up! Please sit down. That chair is very comfortable.'

Sara did so, and unconsciously straightened her sweater. Mrs Conrad handed her a cup of tea and pointed towards the tray with sugar, milk and a plate of biscuits. Sara smiled and took some milk. The room was comfortably furnished with high-quality furniture and decorated in cream, with touches of red. The chosen scheme blended beautifully with the room's Victorian proportions. A cheerful fire was burning in the cast-iron open fireplace. Looking towards the gently dancing flames, Sara spoke.

'How lovely! A real fire — you don't see many of those these days!'

Mrs Conrad nodded.

'We have central heating, but if we know we're going to be home all day, we often turn it off in here and light the fire. It makes a bit of dust, but I think it's worth it because the atmosphere is so cosy and comfortable.'

Sara took a sip of the tea. Trying not to look in James's direction too often, she answered his parent's enquiries about Aunt Margaret, and about how she was coping with running the market garden. She asked about the bell-tower collection and Mrs Conrad told her about the Shrove Tuesday pancake race.

'That's a thought,' she said. 'You'd be an ideal candidate. You will enter, won't you? February the twenty-eighth this year!'

Sara nearly choked on her tea.

'Me? I've never tossed a pancake in my life, and I'm new to the village.'

Waving her hands in the air, Mrs Conrad was already charging ahead and ignoring any emerging resistance.

'The distance end-to-end is two-hundred meters, and you have to toss a pancake three times. I'm sure you could easily manage that. We'd all welcome a new face; the same women take part every year. Go on! Think about it! The money goes towards the church tower. Each competitor needs a sponsor. You'll sponsor Sara, won't you, Jamie?'

There was a silent appeal written in Sara's brown eyes, but it didn't work.

'I'd be delighted!'

A motherly smile covered Mrs Conrad's face, and Sara was sure by the lift of James's eyebrows and his expression that he was actually enjoying her hopeless situation; he knew she was too polite to refuse his mother outright, and guessed that she wouldn't find a suitable excuse fast enough to decline graciously either.

'Good! That's settled then. I'll put your name on the list!'

Steam-rolled, Sara could only close her half-open mouth, and wonder if she could still get out of it without seeming uncivil. Nothing appropriate sprang immediately to mind, and with the seconds quickly passing, and her mind boggling, she resigned herself.

James was sitting in a chair opposite, his long legs stuck out in a straight line, and looking very much relaxed and at home, despite the formal grey suit and conservative maroon tie. He held a cup in his hand and took an occasional sip of tea. The delicate china was lost in his large hand. He leaned forward.

'I did warn you, didn't I?' He said quietly. 'My mother has a powerful flair for manoeuvring people.' His eyes were laughing; his features as he viewed Sara were gentle and contemplative — a fact that wasn't lost on Mrs Conrad.

Resigned, Sara leaned back and tried to ignore the prospect of hurtling along a public road with a pancake in a frying pan. She looked out of the bay window at the beautiful back garden.

'What a big garden, it must need a lot of attention. Who's the gardener?'

'My Dad,' James answered. 'It's his biggest passion!'

'Yes. I'm retired and have lots of time to try new ideas at last,' Mr Conrad joined in. 'My wife helps with weeding and keeping things tidy, so the end result is not all due to my own efforts. Annie's not as interested as I am, but she helps me a lot.'

'I quite enjoy pottering about the garden, if the weather's fine. We both get the benefit out of a nice garden, so I try to do some of the time-consuming bits whenever I can.'

Her husband turned his attention to Sara again.

'If you're really interested, we can take a quick walk around before you leave. There's not very much to see at this time of year, but there is a good show of snowdrops and crocuses, winter jasmine is well on the way, and a couple of other flowering bushes are showing the first signs of colour.'

'Gladly! I spend so much time with vegetables these days, some flowers and a bit of colour would make a welcome change. I love flowers, but I've never tried to grow anything myself. What did you do when you worked?'

'I was a bank manager. It's a far call from gardening, but I was always interested, even then. Gardening is something you like, or something you consider a chore. I like it.'

Sara took a definite partiality to Mr Conrad. He was a quiet man, a gentleman of the old school. He'd clearly been brought up in the belief that being polite and helpful cost nothing. Sara could pick out the same traits mirrored in James. James was a determined businessman, but he hadn't lost the skills of being disciplined and polite while aiming for success. Initial impressions left one with the impression that Mrs Conrad was the bossy one in the family, but that was deceptive. She wouldn't get her way with James, and Sara had the feeling she wouldn't get it with Mr Conrad either — unless he saw a very good reason. Sara had met enough people in her life to decide that all three of them were very likeable in different ways.

Her thoughts were interrupted by the sound of James's cell phone. He lifted his eyebrows and shrugged. Listening for a moment, he answered.

'Well, are you're sure it can't wait?' He looked at his watch. 'I'll meet you there in twenty minutes.' He closed the cell phone with a loud click and got up. 'Sorry, I have to go. Something unexpected has come up at work.'

Sara looked up at his tall figure towering above her and nodded.

'I might call in on the weekend,' he addressed his parents. 'If I do, I'll phone in advance. Perhaps I'll come for supper.'

His mother nodded; clearly, she didn't intend to force him. She probably knew it would have the opposite effect.

He came to his feet smoothly, and when he reached the doorway, he hovered for a moment. Looking back over his shoulder, he said. ''Bye, Sara!'

''Bye!' She lifted her hand.

His mother lifted her hand, too, in farewell and watched him leave. With a speculative look, she reached forward to refill Sara's empty cup.

* * *

Grabbing her car keys and one of Aunt Margaret's lightweight frying pans, Sara drove to the village on Shrove Tuesday feeling nervous and uneasy. The weather wasn't too unpleasant; the sun was trying to break through bundles of dismal grey clouds. Mrs Conrad had given her outlines of how the competitors dressed. She'd plundered her own clothes, and got the rest from her aunt's wardrobe and from her friend, Sandra. She chose a brightly patterned floral apron over a short MacDonald plaid skirt, together with a fluffy green sweater. For safety and comfort, she donned white trainers and pepped them up with bright pink socks adorned with red bows. Tying her hair back with a multi-coloured scarf, she looked at the gaudy reflection in the mirror and wondered if she was completely sane. She might not win, but at least she'd stand out in the crowd.

She parked her car in a side lane, and put her jacket on to walk to the starting line. Sara was surprised how many people had turned out, and she was greeted by smiles and grins when people noticed she was one of the slightly mad competitors. Milling in a circle at the start were several women in similarly colourful attire. She immediately felt a lot better. She spotted Mrs Conrad in the crowd, and pushed her way through to her.

'Will you look after my coat, please?'

Mrs Conrad looked her up and down.

'You look splendid! Yes, of course, give it to me.' Hanging it over her arm, she looked across to where the vicar was trying to call the competitors together. 'You'd better join the others, Sara. The vicar goes through the rules before you get your pancake. Seen James? He's here somewhere. The race starts in ten minutes. Off you go! Good luck!' She laughed softly.

'James? James is here? I thought he'd be too busy!' Her voice trailed off.

'He's a sponsor; he ought to turn up. I saw him earlier with his assistant.'

Sara's heart did a quick somersault. She nodded absentmindedly and turned away. The crowd was spread out along the pavement as far as the church lych-gate. Joining the others, she gave them a chummy smile, and noticed how most of them seemed to be actually enjoying the antics. Clearly, they were used to being the centre of the fun, and didn't mind what they looked like. Brandishing their various frying-pans, they circled around the vicar, who was explaining ther rules.

'The starter shouts 'Frying-pan!', then you toss your pancake high in the air, run to mid-distance, toss the pancake again, and then make a last dash to make a final toss at the finishing line. If anyone drops their pancake they have to give up, or go back to the starting line.' There was a chorus of laughter, and Sara decided she didn't mind larking about with the others — after all, the collection was for a good cause.

The church bell started ringing, each of them was given a rubbery cold pancake for their pans, and they lined up. Sara wetted her lips and looked around. She spotted James, with Pamela at his side, half-way along the course. He was laughing; he lifted his hand and gave her a thumbs-up sign. It was all she could do not to drop the frying-pan before the race began. She pushed him to the back of her mind and concentrated on getting to the finishing line. They heard the starting signal, and then with much cheering and laughter they were off. She tossed her pancake, stuck the pan out in front of her and ran with all her might to mid-way point. She steadied herself and tossed the pancake again. She was pleased she didn't seem to be last; in fact, she was up front at the half-way point. Quickly re-positioning her pancake in the pan again, she made the final dash to the finishing line. She was aware of the wave of encouraging cheers and atmosphere of fun and enjoyment as she went. The crowds trailed after the competitors, filling the road from one side to the other and giving encouraging shouts, all of the last part of the course. At the finishing line, she held her pan with both hands and tossed the pancake again before she darted across the finish. She was aware that the cheering for the winner had started before her pancake was back in the pan, but she was delighted when she realised she'd come in second.

The competitors and spectators gathered around the lych-gate for the presentation. Among loud applause, the winner got an engraved frying-pan from the hands of the vicar. To more accompanying applause, Sara was given a year's supply of eggs from a local farmer and the winner of the third prize got a year's supply of free milk from a local dairy. Sara didn't know what she'd do with a regular amount of eggs, but Aunt Margaret would undoubtedly have good use for them when she got back — she liked baking. With her face still pink from excitement and the unaccustomed exertion, she joined the partakers and onlookers who were heading towards the church hall for tea and cake. She was stopped mid-stream by James's voice.

'Sara! I must say I have seldom seen such an inspiring and elegant vision.' He laughed heartily.

She looked up into his face, picked up the hem of her skirt and did a pirouette. She joined the fun in his expression.

'Which item of my attire catches your connoisseur's eye in particular?'

'It's hard to choose,' he answered, tongue-in-cheek. 'The socks? The frilly knickers? That charming apron? They're all truly awe-inspiring.'

'Yes, I must admit, when I saw myself in the mirror before I left home, I recalled the saying about 'fine feathers make fine birds'.'

He chuckled. 'I think birds would feel insulted and I'd be happier if you hadn't been so successful. I wouldn't need to fork out so much.'

She studied his laughing blue eyes and how the light wind had managed to disrupt his neat hairstyle. 'What will my fantastic performance cost you?'

'As far as I remember, sponsors have to contribute fifty pence per metre for the first, 30 pence for the second, and 25 for the third place. That means my contribution, thanks to you, is sixty quid!'

'Really!' Sara's eyes widened. 'I didn't realize I'd be worth that much!' She was suddenly aware of Pamela glowering at his side. Her expression when she looked at Sara's appearance was of haughty amusement. Pamela would never have taken part in a pancake race — not even for James.

Pamela looked at her watch.

'We have to get back, James! Let's find your mother to say goodbye and get away from all this foolishness!' Without a word of acknowledgement or goodbye to Sara, she turned and was lost in the swarming crowd.

Sara wasn't sorry they were alone. She grabbed his attention for a couple more seconds.

'If I'd known, I'd have tried a lot harder to come first!'

'I see, out to bankrupt me, eh?' He threw back his head slightly and laughed. 'Where did you learn to toss pancakes? It looked very professional.'

She loved the relaxed expression and the laughter in his face. She smiled.

'I asked Jacques to teach me! It took practice, but I got there in the end. I improved my running speed by storming up and down the vegetable trenches, after everyone left for the day. So you see, I did my best not to let my sponsor down, and I didn't. 'Bye, James!' With an upward swirl of her plaid skirt, that showed a hint of the frilly white tennis knickers she'd borrowed from Sandra, she nodded to him and hurried off to join the others streaming into the church hall.

5

With Aunt Margaret's approval, Sara began to re-organize her aunt's office system. She left things that were working well alone and began improving processes that were clogging up the works.

She didn't go to the village very often, but whether she liked it or not, Sara was now part of the community. People remembered her face from the pancake race, especially because she'd come in second. Nowadays, whenever she met somebody in the street, she was greeted by a smile and a friendly word. The baker's shop, with its wonderful fresh bread and pies, was a popular local meeting place. The chocolate éclairs were fantastic; like a handful of thistledown filled with thick cream and covered with a generous layer of milk chocolate. They melted in the mouth.

Sara tried the other cakes, too, but the éclairs remained her favourites, and she had to curb her desire to buy half a dozen every time she was anywhere near the shop. One Friday morning, she met Mrs Conrad talking to another woman in the street.

She smiled and looked at the cake box in Sara's hands.

'Been to Fred's, I see! I was hoping I'd bump into you! I want to ask a favour. This is Radmilla; we're both on the bell-tower committee.'

Sara nodded and smiled at the large, brown-haired woman with glasses at Annie Conrad's side. She was apprehensive about what Mrs Conrad wanted. She didn't want to take part in another public performance if she could avoid it. This time she'd be firm and say no, no matter what it was.

'We need someone to make the posters for the next jumble sale. Someone in the village usually does them for us, but they're on holiday in Australia, and if we don't find a stand-in, we'll have to write them out by hand.'

Sara heaved a silent sigh of relief. This was more in line with her skills.

'How many do you need?'

'Fifty?'

Radmilla, glad of a chance to add to the conversation, explained hastily.

'We try to display plenty of them over a wide area in the hope we'll attract lots and lots of visitors.'

'I'll be glad to help! As long as you only want a normal size sheet of paper; I don't have a special printer for big sheets.'

'No, just the usual thing.' Annie Conrad smiled. 'It would be a great help.'

'My pleasure! Have you decided on the text and what they'll look like?'

'No, not yet. We're going to do that today, or tomorrow afternoon. Tell you what! Why don't you come to supper on Friday? You can pick up our rough copy, and you'll have the chance to ask if anything isn't clear. It'll be a good chance for us to have a chat.'

'Thanks, I'd like that!' Sara said. The prospect of a free meal was enticing.

* * *

Daylight was being swallowed by the night. The first stars were in the heavens and the first quarter of the moon showed it'd be a clear, cold night. As usual, she parked her car on the road outside. It was a habit whenever she visited someone strange. It was easier than having to move her car later for someone to leave, or pass. She walked up the pebble drive, knocked again and waited. Mr Conrad opened the door.

'Hello, Sara! Come in!'

She took-off her hip-length sheepskin jacket; he hung it on the hallstand. She shouldered her bag and fingered the box of chocolates in her hands.

'They're in the living room. You know the way — follow me.'

Sara noted the 'they' and wondered who else was invited — Radmilla? Mr

Conrad preceded her and opened the door. Mrs Conrad stood near the fireplace and James was sitting nearby. Sara hoped her confusion didn't show. Why did she find him so disturbing? He got up.

'My mother told me you were coming, so I invited myself.' He smiled.

'I hope you realize how lucky you are.' She grinned at him. 'My parents are too far away for me to just drop in whenever I like.'

'Would you like a sherry or a glass of wine?' He moved towards the bottles and glasses on the nearby sideboard. 'Where do your parents live?'

'A glass of wine, please. Near Gloucester. Dad owns a small electrical business, and Mum helps him out with the office work, and organizes everything else. I have an older brother who lives and works in Bristol.' Sara wondered why she felt only he and she were in the room. She made a deliberate attempt to focus on Mrs Conrad who was studying them with particular interest.

'Thank you for the invitation, Mrs Conrad.' She handed her the chocolates. 'I hope you'll like these.'

'I'm sure I will!' James answered for her.

Sara turned to him.

'They're not for you.' She looked at Mrs Conrad. 'Make sure he doesn't get any. He can afford to buy his own!'

'It's kind of you, but quite unnecessary,' Mrs Conrad accepted the box and smiled indulgently. 'You're doing me a favour, not the other way round.'

Sara's eyes sparkled and she accepted a long-stemmed crystal glass and looked around. The light floral chintz curtains framing the windows were one of the room's outstanding features; luxurious in length, the smooth, shiny texture looked completely contemporary. They complimented the fine classical furniture in the room very well.

Mrs Conrad put the box down on a nearby table.

'Let's go straight in and have our

meal, shall we?' she said. 'I can show you our idea for the jumble sale poster later on.'

The food was delicious and very enjoyable. They had Parma ham with melon, a rich lasagne with a side salad, and some tiramisu to finish the meal. James's parents were good hosts, and for some reason she had a feeling James's presence this evening made everything twice as pleasing for her. After they'd finished their coffee, they all returned to the sitting room. Mr Conrad prodded the fire into life again and Mrs Conrad fetched Sara the outline for the poster. It was straightforward and there was little to query. Sara folded it and put it in her bag. James chatted to his father and put on a CD. Sara sensed that the two men got on well. He got on with his mother, too, and clearly detached himself from her, without it damaging their rapport. They'd come to terms, and learned to accept each other as they were.

In the grate, the fire crackled. The flames picked out the chestnut highlights in Sara's hair and danced on her cherry red sweater before finally losing themselves in its soft folds. She sat in an armchair on one side of the fireside; her slim legs in her narrow black trousers neatly crossed. Sara recognized Mozart in the background; the music flowed softly and quietly, not intruding on the conversation. She joined in the ripple of conversation about the village and its inhabitants, or about other themes that came up. She tried not to look in James's direction too often, although he seemed to drag her interest like a pin drawn to a magnet. When she glanced at her watch, she was surprised how quickly the time had passed.

James's cell phone rang. He searched impatiently in an inner pocket of the casual suede jacket he was wearing and they all waited silently.

'Yes.' His voice was curt. The expression on his face lengthened. 'Surely it can wait until tomorrow?' He was silent. 'Oh, very well I'll call on the way home and check things.' He continued to listen. 'Yes, I do know that it closes at ten-thirty, but someone will be in the kitchen after that — clearing up. I'll let you know on Monday.' With a click, he cut the connection, and stood up. 'That was Pamela. One of our customers is playing up because frozen lamb we delivered today arrived partly thawed. I can't imagine how that could happen. Everything is stored properly until it's delivered, and Pamela only sends it on its way when she's sure it will arrive in perfect condition.' Clearly irritated by the disruption, he moved towards the door. 'See you next week sometime, Mum. 'Bye Sara!'

Sara pushed herself to a standing position.

'It's been a lovely evening, but I think it's time for me to leave, too.'

'Must you?' Mrs Conrad looked disappointed. 'You don't have to go just because James is leaving. It was such a pleasant evening till now.'

'I agree,' Sara added. 'But we'd have called it a day soon anyway. I really enjoyed the evening and the meal; thank you very much!'

Once Sara and James were in their coats, they all said their goodbyes and when the door closed on them, they walked down the driveway. James insisted on walking with her to her car. They wandered past his own, tucked in at the side of his father's garage.

She unlocked the car door, and with one hand still in his pocket, to her utter surprise, he leaned forward and kissed her cheek fleetingly.

'Goodnight! Safe journey!'

Surprised, she somehow managed to answer, 'You, too! Goodnight!'

He turned and strode purposely back up the driveway. She revved the engine and drew smoothly away from the pavement. In the mirror, she saw his car disappearing in the opposite direction. She touched the spot where his lips had brushed her cheek, and she experienced an array of perplexing emotions. She refused to believe it meant anything; he was just being polite — lots of people kissed each other's cheeks these days. Her thoughts scampered restlessly around on the journey home, and after she'd locked up for the night, she was still puzzled. It had unnerved her a little.

* * *

Even though the worst of the winter was over, it didn't mean an outbreak of flu could be avoided. First, both temporary helpers phoned to say they were ill; then the two full-time gardeners came down with the same symptoms. Things still ticked over with Bill and a trainee worker shouldering the burden. Sara joined in and worked alongside them in the sheds; helping with the packing. On Friday morning, she noticed that Bill looked feverish. He even complained of the cold when he arrived; something he'd never done before. After a cup of tea in the office, he wrapped his scotch-plaid scarf tighter round his neck and set off to tackle his day's work.

If they got through today without too many difficulties, there'd be a brief respite over the weekend and there was hope one of the full-time workers would be back on Monday. She checked the incoming mail, answered emails, worked out the orders for the beginning of the coming week. It was past lunchtime and fluffy white clouds were scurrying across the sky. Switching on the answering machine, and slipping into her anorak, she went to look for Bill. He and Robbie, the trainee, were standing in the trenches busy digging up kale at the far end of the garden. Leaning on his spade, Bill was wiping the sweat from his brow and he looked as pale as a ghost. Sara felt worried. His eyes were feverish; he was clearly feeling ghastly.

She took the spade off him as he straightened up.

'Bill, you're ill. Go to the doctor's

now, before he closes, and then home to a warm bed and some rest. If you don't, you'll end up with pneumonia or worse and then you'll be off work for weeks instead of a day or two.'

'I can't go home now,' he replied. 'We have orders for Conrad and Coleman. We promised delivery by six.'

'How much do we still have to dig?'

'At a guess.' He glanced down the field. 'This row, down to the leeks!'

'Right! Show me how to get one out undamaged and then go home! Robbie and I will manage, won't we, Robbie?' The young man looked taken aback, but he nodded.

'It's not just lifting them — they have to be sorted, washed and packed.'

'We'll manage! I've sorted and prepared things for packing before. Show me and then get off home!'

Reluctantly he gave in. When he saw she could manage, he wiped his brow again, and with Sara's wishes for a speedy recovery and several regretful back glances, he left. He dragged himself sluggishly towards his slightly dilapidated car. A few minutes later, she heard it spring reluctantly to life and saw it move in the direction of the village. Sara knew he must feel very ill to have given in.

She straightened up.

'I'm going back to the house to change into some warmer clothes and get some gloves. I'll take this lot back with me to the shed on the way.'

Robbie nodded.

'How long will we need?'

He shrugged and looked up at the sky.

'An hour? Two, perhaps! You have to be careful with bio-vegetables. If they get damaged, customers complain something awful.'

Even before she got back to the packing shed, her hands were cold. She hurried, dressing in her oldest, warmest clothes, and then unloading the contents of the wheelbarrow into the washing troughs before she returned to Robbie. On the way out, she checked the list pinned to the wall to see how much, and which vegetables they needed. After only half-an-hour, her back was aching from the unaccustomed work, and the cold wind was making short-work of her warm clothing. The earth was heavy, soaked by recent rain. It made lifting very arduous, but every kale in the wheelbarrow was a step nearer their goal. Robbie was used to the conditions and work, and he was oblivious of Sara's discomfort. There was no time for companionable chats. Now and then, she was glad to break off from digging — even if it was just to push the filled wheelbarrow back to the shed and unload it. It was half past four when they finally finished outside.

'It's time for you to knock off work, Robbie!' She looked at her watch.

'Yes, but I'll stay a bit longer; help you get the parsnip and carrots from storage, and fetch the radishes and the spring onions from the glasshouses.'

Sara nodded gratefully. If Robbie

helped with the other vegetables, then she'd be free to start washing and packing the kale straight away, and she'd be able to move on to the other things when that was finished.

* * *

It was quiet in the shed. Robbie had left, and she stopped looking at her watch because it only made her more nervous. With the requirement lists for Coleman and Conrad in front of her, she was busily washing, sorting and packing. Coleman's order was finished. The boxes were stacked neatly on one side, and she'd started on Conrad's order. Her hands were like blocks of ice. The water was already very cold coming out of the tap, and felt even icier when she held the vegetables under the stream of water to remove any mud. Even after gently shaking them, she had to leave them to drip-dry for a while. Luckily, the boxes were lined with plastic, but she couldn't risk packing them in a pool of water.

She thought longingly about a comforting hot drink, a warm bath and creeping into bed with an electric blanket, but that had to wait a while yet. Daylight was fading fast and she was now forced to work by the overhead lighting. She heard a car drawing up outside but didn't stop. A few minutes later the door squeaked as the rusty hinges gave way and it opened to let in yet another gust of cold wind. His curt voice lashed out at her. She didn't need to look up to know it was James.

'What the devil is going on? Do you realise I'm waiting for my order?'

She noted the set face, the clamped mouth and fixed eyes; his expression sent her temper soaring.

'Nice to see you, too, James! You don't need to remind me; I know you're waiting for your order.'

'Then will you explain where it is?' The angry retort hardened his features and he looked down at the metal casing of his wrist watch. 'It was supposed to be delivered at our place at least an hour ago! I hope you're not under the misguided belief that I'll make excuses for shoddy business practices just because we've met socially a couple of times?' His cold eyes sniped at her.

She set her chin in a stubborn line and flashed him a look of sheer anger in return.

'No, I don't suppose you'd do that. Business always comes first in your world, doesn't it?' Her breath burned in her throat and tears were threatening at the back of her eyes, but she kept them under control. There was silence between them, and he stood there looking tall and angry. She looked away and concentrated on packing a box with fat turnips.

'Where are the others?' he asked, noticing the lack of noise in the shed.

'There are no others; it's just me.' She turned back to packing the next box, after referring briefly to the list on the table in front of her. She decided he was entitled to an explanation. 'Bill went home this morning; he was ill. The other workers are already off with flu. Our trainee worker, Robbie helped me get the stuff out of the garden and in here for packing. He left ten minutes ago to catch his bus, if he hadn't gone now he'd have to hang around for another two hours. I'm almost finished; just a couple more minutes and everything will be ready. You can wait in the office if you want to make sure the order is finished; it's warmer in there. I know that we have a contract to deliver the vegetables on time, but I'm hoping that you'll make an exception for us today and accept the hold-up. I should have phoned, but I haven't been indoors since lunchtime because I didn't want to interrupt the work; I hoped that we'd make it on time.' Her breath burned in her throat. 'I've got to deliver an order to Coleman's, too, but I'll deliver yours first.' She bit her lip. 'I apologise for the delay, but I hope that under the circumstances you'll understand.' The long deep look he gave her infuriated her even more.

He studied her more closely and noticed the pinched lips, white face and red hands. Even though she was dressed warmly in outlandish looking clothes, if she'd been out in the garden digging and then cleaning and packing the vegetables in this icebox of a shed, she must be frozen to the core by now. He ran his hands through his hair and tried to back pedal.

'I tried to phone you — several times — to find out what was happening, but only got the answering machine. Then I started to get nervous because the order is for one of our most important customers, I thought you'd forgotten it.' He won no answering smile. He waved his hands vaguely around. 'Now I'm here and know what's happened, can I help?'

Her voice was as icy as her body.

'No, thank you. Coleman's order is finished, and yours will be ready in roughly ten minutes.'

'Where's the order for Coleman?'

'Over there.' She nodded to the stacked boxes on the floor by the door.

'Give me the keys to the van. I'll load the order and deliver it, and come back for my stuff after.'

Disconcerted, she crossed her arms and looked at him with a mountain of emotions hacking away at her insides.

'I'll deliver the goods; it's part of the contract.'

His grey eyes darkened to a shade of granite and his expression was severe.

'Don't be stubborn, Sara. You need a helping hand, and I'm offering you one. I didn't know what the situation was; otherwise I wouldn't have attacked you.'

Under his steady scrutiny, she was unnerved and needed a moment to re-orientate herself. She lowered her gaze and was silent. She knew she had to take a step towards him or their frail friendship might disintegrate and she didn't want that to happen. Her brown eyes darkened, looked almost black as with blinding certainty she realised that she was in love with this man. She struggled with the knowledge, aware now that despite his rough edges, he was the 'special someone' she'd searched for all her life. She opened her mouth and shut it as her breath caught in her lungs. Every time his gaze met hers, her heart turned over in an eloquent response and she felt like a breathless girl of eighteen.

Finally, she nodded silently and rummaged in her pocket for the bunch of keys. She ruffled through them when they were lying in her palm until she found the right one. Holding it between her fingers, she handed it to him, careful not to let her fingers touch his.

'The delivery note is on the top one.' Her voice felt wobbly. 'Do you know where Coleman's is?'

He nodded.

'Of course. Tradesman's entrance . . . ? Right! If I'm recognised, I'll never live it down!'

Sara was entirely caught up in her own emotions, but managed somehow to reply and sound natural.

'They won't; who'd expect the manager of a well-known company to act as delivery boy!' She gave him a weak smile. 'Thanks, James!'

'Don't worry . . . I have an old coat in the boot of the car. I'll get it, load the boxes and be off. When you're finished, leave my stuff stacked where it is and get yourself warmed up indoors. A hot drink and a bath will set you up again. When I come back, I'll load my stuff, leave my car here overnight, and pick it up tomorrow morning. Is that okay with you?'

'Yes, of course!' she said, grateful beyond words for his help.

He turned and strode towards the door. Sara returned to finish packing the rest of his order; contented in the knowledge that she could now look forward to some warmth and shelter indoors, and that James had turned out to be her knight in white armour.

Once she was indoors, Sara was so tired, after she'd made herself a warm drink and had a hot bath, she just crept into bed and pulled the duvet up to her neck and fell into a dreamless sleep.

6

Rays of sunlight sneaked past the open curtains and nestled among the folds of the bedclothes. Sara looked up at the ceiling and stretched her arms above her head. Sore muscles complained from her shoulders to the calves of her legs. She mused that she must have more muscles than she realized; lots of them were tetchy and disagreeable ones, too. Looking at the clock, she dragged herself, aching pains and all, out of bed. Heavens! It was nine-thirty! Then she remembered yesterday, and that it was Saturday; she relaxed again.

With awkward manoeuvring, she thrust her arms into her dressing gown, searched for her slippers with her toes, and went to the bathroom. She was glad that she hadn't caught a cold — something she expected after the previous day. Downstairs, she put the kettle on and picked up the morning paper. The phone rang; it was Jenny, Bill's wife.

'Sorry to bother you so early but he won't give me any peace until I find out if things worked out yesterday!'

'We missed him, but we managed. How is he? Did he go to the doctor?'

'Yes, he must have felt bad; he hasn't been there for years. The doctor prescribed antibiotics and sent him home to bed.'

'And? Is he feeling better?'

'Yes, thank goodness. His temperature has gone down, and he's much recovered. I'll have my work cut out to keep him here on Monday.'

'He is not to come back until the doctor says he can! One of the other full-timers is back on Monday, and at the moment there are no orders that'll be waiting to go out.'

Jenny sounded reassured.

'That's good! Can I tell him he can phone you on Monday? It'll help me keep him under control!'

'If it helps!' Sara laughed. 'I'll only tell him I don't want him back until he's fit!'

* * *

She was famished. She took some bacon and eggs out of the fridge and began to cook breakfast. When a knock on the back door shattered her solitary state, she pushed the pan to the side of the cooker and, clutching the collar of her dressing-gown, she went to see who it was.

'James, what are you doing here?' She stared at him, breathless.

Dangling the set of van keys in front of her, he hovered in the doorway.

'I had to bring back the van, and pick up my car, remember?' He looked her over seductively. 'I must say you look attractive this morning.'

She coloured lightly, aware of her tousled hair and appearance. Leaning against the doorframe for a moment, she gathered enough strength to reply.

'Oh yes, your car! I forgot. Did your order get there on time?'

'Yes! No problem!' His nose wrinkled and he sniffed. 'That smells good.'

'Like to join me?' She asked, not expecting that he would.

'Honest? I haven't had breakfast yet. It's very tempting.'

'I'll get dressed and be back in a jiff.' She opened the door and gestured him in.

He shook his head.

'You weren't intending to dress for breakfast, so don't bother to do so for me! You look perfectly respectable, and very eye-catching.' He was past her, taking off his coat, and throwing it over a nearby chair all in one fluid movement. Before she had time to close her mouth, he was positioned in front of the cooker. 'I'll do the cooking, where are the plates?'

'I'll get them. Coffee or tea?'

'I don't mind, but to be honest, I'd prefer coffee.'

'Toast and marmalade?'

'Please!' He nodded and grinned.

Ten minutes later, with the aroma of fried bacon and coffee circling around, they sat opposite each other with half-empty plates. Sara held a cup between her hands.

'Isn't it great to have a proper breakfast? Do you always have one?'

'Not really I make do with cereal or a couple of pieces of toast and instant coffee.' He took a healthy bite of his toast and began to chew with obvious relish.

'I'm roughly the same; it has to be quick and nourishing! My aunt has a cleaning lady, so I'm having a fairly luxurious time. Normally I do mundane things like shopping, housework and my washing on Saturday. I try to keep Sunday free to laze around.' She forked the last bit of bacon and dragged it through the egg yolk left on her plate. 'I can't imagine you lazing around!'

He smiled a crooked smile and sipped coffee. Sara's attention was drawn to his long fingers wrapped around the cup.

'I assure you I can, and do laze around; reading, watching sport; the kind of things most other people do on the weekend.' He put the cup down and leaned back contentedly, stretching his arms behind his head; his flannel shirt pulled tightly across his chest. 'That was good. Thank you for inviting me.'

'You're welcome. You did the cooking anyway!' Sara was unaware of the attractive picture she made. Bereft of make-up, the colour of her pink dressing gown was tingeing the creamy surface of her skin, her waist was defined by the tight belt, and a relaxed and contented expression covered her face. She smiled at him and tried to store the memory of this moment. Nothing could be more agreeable than sharing breakfast with someone you loved.

'What are you doing today?' He asked speculatively.

'I haven't decided.' She wrinkled her nose. 'Once I've dressed, I'll have to clear up the chaos I left in the shed. I was thinking of going to the cinema this evening. There's a Meryl Streep film I want to see. I'm going home for the day tomorrow.'

'Yes, I saw it advertised; it's had good reviews. Going with someone?'

'I was going to phone my friend Sandra. See if she was free.'

He studied her face.

'Perhaps we can go together? Unless you'd rather go with your friend . . . '

Sara was dumbstruck for the moment. She felt like a teenager being asked out on a date by someone she'd made sheep's eyes at for weeks and months. She swallowed a lump in her throat and hoped she sounded casual.

'I'd like that.'

'Good.' He got up. Sara had the feeling he almost touched the ceiling. 'Shall I pick you up?'

'No, we go in your direction anyway don't we? I'll pick you up.'

* * *

She spent ages getting ready. Her freshly-washed hair gleamed like burnished copper. Her knee-length, dark-lavender tunic dress skimmed her figure. She'd taken special care with her make-up, and her high-heels showed off her legs to perfection. Her eyes were dark with anticipation and she felt blissfully happy.

Sara set off with time to spare. It was still a few hours till daylight faded completely and she surveyed the narrow main road carefully, trying to catch a glimpse of the turn-off from the main road. When she found it, she reduced speed and turned the corner smoothly. The back-road was bordered by high hedges and it had ragged trees with intertwining branches high above; it was like driving through a tunnel. A matter of minutes later she reached the open five-bar gate, with the name *Wayside* written in white on an oval black plaque. She drove up the slightly curving track towards the house.

When she came in sight of it, she was

facing an ultra-modern box-shaped building. The entrance door was to the right, in a recessed open patio supported by narrow, straight columns. The outside was greyish-beige and several narrow windows broke up the straight-lined façade. An unadorned lawn stretched in front of the building; unadorned except for a stone that looked like a miniature menhir positioned on one side. She wondered if it had always been there or intentionally placed for the impact it made. Some twisting evergreen plants climbed the columns to break the total severity, but the unembellished lines of the house continued to dominate the senses. Even her untrained eye could tell the house must have cost a fortune.

She pocketed her keys and got out. Looking around the immediate surroundings, she couldn't see any other buildings. A bird was singing nearby and a light breeze rustled the leaves in the trees and blew her hair in disarray. Patting it back into shape, she rang the bell, and heard footsteps. James opened the door and smiled at her. He looked relaxed and at ease with himself. The sleeves of his blue checked shirt were rolled neatly up to his elbows, and he sported 5-pocket-jeans that hugged his hips hungrily.

His eyes skimmed her appearance and he gave her an admiring look.

'No wellingtons? I must say I like this new style very much. Come in!'

There was a smell of freshly-ground coffee floating around as she followed him through a large square-shaped hall towards the back of the building. The floor was terracotta tiling; some bright, modern pictures hung on the rough-plastered cream walls, and a smooth, intertwined modern sculpture stood on a dark side table. The sound of her heels echoed as they went along. There were doorframes, but no doors. When they reached it, the living room ran the length of the back of the house and overlooked a long stone terrace. Dotted along it were over-sized unglazed containers with evergreen plants. Even in the fading light, Sara could see a fantastic view through the floor-to-ceiling windows. In summer, the sun would shine generously on the terrazzo. On this side of the house, they were elevated. The mound descended and blended with the shadowed terrain below. She searched for his face; needing to comment on what she thought, and found he was watching her.

'Wow! It's the kind of house I've seen in architect and design magazines; it's definitely not typical for this area, is it?'

'What did you expect?'

'I don't know; anything from a country cottage, to a big house with dormer windows and pillared entrance, or perhaps a sprawling mansion!'

He laughed, the lines deepening.

'And?' he enquired in a voice of muted velvet.

She looked around at the sparsely-furnished room

'I like it! Everything is minimal

design but with maximum effect.'

'There's always room for improvement!' he added, clearly pleased.

'I'm sure if you marry, your wife will want to add some decorative touches, like plants, or perhaps a bit more colour — women always do, but if she's clever she won't spoil what you've already achieved. It's really lovely!'

He ran his fingers through his hair.

'I couldn't live with horse-brasses or rocking chairs, but I wouldn't object to anything which gives the house the atmosphere of a real home. The cottage in Brittany I was telling you about, is the complete opposite of this. It's over a hundred years old, with small rooms, hardly any garden, tiny windows. Both houses are special in very different ways.'

'Did an architect design this? I suppose so!'

'Indirectly; I saw a house like this in Spain years ago, and vowed that if I ever had enough money, I'd build one like it. I showed my architect the photos, and he used the basic idea to make the plans for this.'

She glanced out of the windows again.

'You don't seem to have any neighbours?'

He pointed.

'It might look so, but there's a farm over there, and a couple of cottages among the trees down the bottom of the slope. Just around the corner, you can't see it from here, there's an old parsonage. A young couple moved in there recently. I'm not completely cut off from neighbours but, admittedly, it is very quiet here. There used to be a small cottage on this spot, and when I saw it was up for sale, I decided it was the ideal place to build if I could get planning permission. If I was closer to the town, I might have faced a lot more opposition from the planning authorities, but a young chap handled my application and he was extremely helpful and supportive. The cottage was removed and this was built on the spot instead. I'm not far from the main road; it only gets a little tricky when there's ice or snow, but that doesn't happen often and I've an old four-wheel-drive in the garage that can cope with any adverse conditions like that.' He stuck his hands in his pockets.

'What do your parents say about it? They have a very down-to-earth house in comparison to this.'

He tilted his head to the side.

'My mother would like to add fitted carpets and put curtains on all the windows; my father is dying to string tidy flower beds down the hillside and plant high bushes in a straight line in front of the terrace — to ensure privacy!'

'Oh, no!' She laughed. 'Really?'

'Honestly! They mean well, but I think they're gradually adjusting to the fact that I want my home to be as open and as natural as possible!'

'I like your parents.'

'Do you? Good! They're decent sorts, even if I say so! Like a coffee?'

'Yes, we still have plenty of time.'

He wandered off and Sara sat down in one of the armchairs to await his return; she salted away the details of what she could see around her. He came back with two black mugs; put one down in front of her.

'Milk, no sugar, okay?'

'Just right! Thanks!' She smiled. 'You have a good memory!'

He sat down and leaned back contentedly, still holding his mug of coffee.

'We need roughly fifteen to twenty minutes to get to the cinema. My car or yours?'

'If you don't mind riding in an old Ford, we'll take mine . . . '

Sara expected to remember the evening, and did. She was flustered just to be with him, and afterwards she couldn't properly recollect what the film was about. She was only aware of being with James. Next to him in the darkness, with the screen flashing moments of brightness, she looked at him out of the corner of her eye. He seemed very absorbed in the film, and she pulled herself together — but there was something wonderful about being cocooned in the warm anonymity of cinema seats in dark obscurity together with the man she loved.

On the way home, they talked about the film. Sara couldn't remember a lot of the plot, but found she'd remembered enough to comment in the right way: With a giddy sense of pleasure, she let her happiness take over and just enjoyed his closeness. The headlights cut through the night and the return journey didn't take long enough. She drove up the driveway; the wheels crunched on the pebbles in the stillness of the night. Above them, the sky was a blanket of stars in a velvet sky.

'Would you like to come in for a drink?'

'No, thanks,' she said, although she was tempted. 'I'm going home to see my parents tomorrow: that means I have to make an early start.'

He nodded. If he had hoped for another answer, he didn't show it.

'Oh yes, you mentioned that this morning. Well, have a safe journey. It's a long way to go for the day.'

'I intended to go for the weekend, but changed plans when Bill was taken ill. I haven't been home for months, and I don't want to disappoint them again. I have to make the effort. Normally I would stay till Monday and come back Tuesday, but at the moment that isn't a good idea either — a couple of people are off ill and I should be there just in case!'

He nodded understandingly.

'We'll be in touch?'

'Of course!' She hesitated for a moment, studying the outline of his silhouette in the darkness. Sara wished she knew him well enough to guess what he was thinking. If she'd agreed to stay, would it have gone further than a cup of coffee . . . ?

Suddenly he stretched his arm across the back of her seat and leaned forward to kiss her. The kiss was slow, thoughtful. The caress on her lips set her aflame and she drank in the sweetness. She breathed lightly between parted lips as he turned away and opened the door. When he was standing in the sparse moonlight he slammed the door, and she pulled herself together. She reversed down the drive. There was still a tantalizing smell of his aftershave and she wished she could save it in a bottle. The headlights lit up the surroundings when she looked back briefly. He lifted a hand and she waved back, though she wasn't sure if he saw her. He turned and went towards the door. Her heart was still hammering foolishly and the pit of her stomach was churning. A kiss from someone you loved, however innocently given, was not something to take lightly or something to forget easily.

7

A week later, Bill was back at work. He looked better and insisted that he felt top-fit. Sara took a few hours off to go into Hockingdale. She wanted to go to the chemist's, buy some stamps, and visit the hairdressers.

Her hair newly trimmed, and with some up-to-the-minute lipstick and favourite shampoo in her shopping bag, she went on towards the post-office. She wasn't looking for, or expecting to see, any familiar faces, so she was a little startled when someone called her name and she turned to find it was Jenny. From their brief telephone conversations and chats in the village shop, Sara already liked her. Jenny had a friendly round face, soft dark eyes, and a comfortable, kindly manner.

'Hello, Jenny! Sorry, I never expect to

meet anyone that I know here. How are you?'

'I'm fine thanks, and you?' Jenny smiled. 'I think you'd be surprised how many people know you; we're a nosey lot in the village! Since the pancake race most people know your face.

'Are you shopping? Want a lift back? I'm on my way to the post office, but I'll be going straight home again after that.'

'That's kind of you, but I came to change my library books, and then I'm going to see my sister-in-law for a cup of tea and a gossip.'

Sara nodded and her forehead wrinkled as she said.

'Actually, I'm glad we've met. It gives me the chance to ask if Bill is really fit. He says he is, but I hope he's not pushing himself because he feels he's got to, for the sake of the market garden!'

Jenny shook her head.

'No, don't worry! The doctor says as long as Bill feels he can cope, it's okay.

If I tried to keep him indoors, it'd drive him mad. He's not one to sit around reading or doing the like. As long as he doesn't take any stupid risks, he'll be all right. And he's promised me he won't do that!'

Sara was relieved. Without noticing, Sara discovered they were chatting outside Ken's bookshop. He rapped the window to catch their attention, nodded to Bill's wife, and hooked his finger motioning Sara to come in. He had to vanish again, probably to serve a customer.

Jenny's lively expression changed to one of obvious surprise.

'Is Ken expecting you?'

Sara shook her head. 'No not really, he's just seen us and I expect he isn't busy at the moment. I've only met him once or twice.'

Jenny looked towards the shop and sniffed.

'I've lost count how many girlfriends he's had in the last couple of years. You quite often get the impression he is a bit of a Casanova, to be honest.'

Sara was intrigued.

'He was a friend of your son's and of James Conrad wasn't he?'

'Yes, a long time ago. Ken's not a bad sort, really, but sometimes he's also his own worst enemy.'

'When I was with the two of them recently there was tension in the air. Was it my imagination, or is there a reason?'

'I suppose I shouldn't gossip,' Jenny began tentatively. 'But it's ancient knowledge in the village . . . No — you didn't imagine that something was wrong. A group of village boys, including James, Tony, and our Martin, were great pals all through their childhood. I can't remember how old they were when it fell apart — they were perhaps fourteen, or fifteen. James had a girlfriend — he was the only one at that time, and for teenage boys, having a girlfriend meant prestige and status among your friends! She was a pretty little thing from a neighbouring village. One day some devil prompted Ken to steal her away, even though he wasn't really interested himself. He probably didn't think about the consequences, of course, but that ended any pretence of friendship. Trust and fellowship went down the drain; and the others steered clear of Ken after that, not just James. They pass the time of day, but there's no love lost between them anymore.'

Sara listened and frowned.

'Oh, I see! Even if it was a long time ago, it's easy to understand why James ignored him after that, isn't it?' Jenny nodded and Sara continued. 'In a small village with only a couple of teenage boys of the same age it was a pretty stupid thing to do. No genuine friend would do something like that — not for fun and not as a dare either. If my best friend had pinched my boyfriend, I'd have torn her hair out, strand by strand!'

Jenny laughed, 'Women react differently. Perhaps Ken couldn't help himself; but it revealed his true character. He hasn't changed much — I don't mean that he's intentionally wilful or thoughtless, but sometimes he gets carried away and doesn't stop to think what the long-term outcome of his actions will be. He can charm the birds off the trees, but the impulsive side of his character makes him unpredictable. Ken dropped out of the gang when he noticed things had backfired and the others in the group began to shun his company most of the time. I think that's why he ended up opening a shop here. Most of the other boys are still good friends; they see one another if they're visiting parents at Christmas, that sort of thing!'

'What about the girl?'

Jenny shrugged her shoulders.

'Apparently she's an actress now. Someone told me they'd seen her in a supporting role on the TV. I do know that her family moved from the area years and years ago. Silly girl! Even if she was a gullible teenager, who'd be daft enough to give up James for someone like Ken?' Jenny adjusted the weight of the plastic bag in her hand. 'Luckily it didn't put James off girlfriends forever.' She smiled and laughed.

'He doesn't seem the flirting kind.' Sara couldn't help herself.

'He isn't, but there have been some — as far as I know nothing serious so far. I like James; I always have. He's a very steady character and I can imagine he often has trouble adjusting to the ideas some girls have nowadays. A lot of modern young women have plan B tucked away at the back of their drawer, before they've even bought their wedding dress. A fly-by-night wouldn't suit him at all.'

Sara smiled and Jenny looked at Ken's book shop again briefly.

'Well, I must get on! Maureen will be wondering where I am. I've already spent too long in the library, and now I'm gossiping the time away with you again! Don't worry about Bill. I'm watching him.'

'Without Bill, I wouldn't stand a chance. He's the backbone of the place! Enjoy your chat.' Sara hoisted her shoulder bag. ''Bye!'

''Bye, dear. Send our best wishes to Maggie when you speak to her!'

'I will.'

They parted company and went off in opposite directions. Sara walked on towards the newsagent-cum-post-office at the end of the street. After listening to Jenny, she deliberated whether or not to ignore Ken, but she wanted to be sensible and fair. The trouble between James and Ken was none of her business. It diminished Ken's standing in her eyes, because she loved James — and anything that bothered him, bothered her — but Ken had always been friendly, and never overstepped the mark. There was no honest reason why she ought to ignore him completely. She decided to call in the bookshop briefly on the way back.

Stamps and stamped-envelopes bought and stored away, she retraced her steps and drew level with the window display. She studied the books on offer, and decided he knew his job, however wide of the mark he'd been with James. With her hand on the doorknob, she heard someone sound the horn and looked up to see James's car drawing level. Smiling, she waved to him. The shop door opened and Ken stood expectantly in the entrance. Looking at Sara, and then in the direction she'd been waving, he dropped an arm casually round her shoulder, waved offhandedly to James, and drew her inside. Sara didn't see his expression and hostile glare.

Ken brought her some coffee and they sat in one of the comfortable corners. It was fairly quiet in the shop and Ken only left her to serve someone at the counter now and then. Between times, he leaned back with his hands crossed behind his head; his legs stuck out in front of him. Clearly he was satisfied with his lot in life. The two of them chatted easily for a while. His corduroy slacks, soft loafers and check flannel shirt suited his surroundings, his job, and his attitude perfectly. Sara made appropriate remarks about how she liked his shop. He told her about the first couple of years, when he wasn't sure if he'd survive, and how he now had a steady stream of loyal customers and a fairly stable income. He could now afford the occasional trip abroad and other things that weren't possible a few years ago, when his income just about covered his daily needs.

'Do you live in Hockingdale?' she asked politely.

'Yes, I live here, in fact, in the flat over the shop. In many ways, it's very convenient. No travelling back and forth, and if something urgent crops up, I can easily put up a notice to say 'back in half-an-hour'!'

'Do you own it — the shop?' She floundered for a moment. 'Oh, I suppose I shouldn't be so nosey.'

'Why ever not — it's no secret! I didn't intend to buy the place when I started out, but the bank-manager persuaded me that was the way to go. He said a bank would be more sympathetic in times of an emergency. It was good advice; and I'm not sorry I did it now. The place will be entirely mine in a couple of years. I never thought I'd ever aim for security, but perhaps I'm growing older and wiser?' He smiled and shrugged. 'Anyway, once I've paid off the mortgage, my overheads will nose-dive and I'll have a lot more financial freedom.'

Sara looked amused.

'And then you'll open another bookshop, in the village?'

He linked his hands behind his head.

'Perhaps! Although it would be infinitely more sensible to concentrate on this place and enjoy life. I wouldn't want to sell it, not when it's beginning to pay off at last, so if I had another shop in the village, I'd have to employ someone to work full-time, here or there. That, and paying for the new shop, would swallow the profits for years and years, and I'm not yet convinced it would be worth the effort. This place will provide me with a very good lifestyle if I concentrate on improving and expanding. I could always buy a flat or a house, and include the upstairs rooms into the shop if I wanted to expand. I'll see how things go, and what things are like in a couple of years.'

Even though she knew the reason for the tension between him and James, there was something about Ken that she couldn't dislike. He wasn't an irresponsible businessman, so perhaps he had become a more sensible character with the passing of time. She drank the last dregs from the mug of coffee, looked at her watch and pushed herself to her feet.

'I must get back; I only intended to make a quick trip.'

He viewed her intensely, admiring the attractive face and liking her open friendliness. He stood up and held out his hand. She let him pull her to her feet.

'Thanks for the coffee!' she said.

'You're welcome!' He smiled. 'Next time you come, phone me first. Women have a bizarre interest in seeing where you live. I'll show you my flat — but only if I get a pre-warning so that I can pick the socks and the underwear up off the floor first! Perhaps we can have a bit of lunch together in the pub down the road?'

'I don't suppose that your flat is full of etchings by any chance?'

He laughed.

'Wow! My dear girl, that is completely outdated these days. Men currently use the magnetism of things like favourite CDs, wine collections, much-loved videos. You'd never believe the number of girls who are prepared to watch *Pride and Prejudice* for the tenth time!! But if I had designs on you, I think I'd have to find something better than that, wouldn't I?' There was a speculative look on his face.

'A lot better!'

'Thought so.' He grinned. 'But the

invitation stands!'

'I'll remember!' Bantering in a relaxed manner, she smiled.

She strolled through the streets back to the car-park. In one of the arched break-way into the dry stonework wall surrounding the car-park, she came face to face with James. His tall figure stopped midstride when he saw her and she automatically slowed to a halt as well. Her delight at seeing him fired the usual feeling of bubbling exhilaration somewhere inside. She'd just left Ken and it was like leaving the desert and coming across an oasis.

'Hi!' It was no effort for her to smile at him, but she was surprised to find her smile wasn't returned.

His hands were stuffed deeply in the pockets of his dark coat. A fine wool scarf was draped loosely around his neck, and the light breezes were bringing his hair into disarray. He looked at her with a stern expression on his face and merely nodded a greeting.

Sensing he wasn't going to start up

the conversation, she did.

'Are you here on business, or on pleasure?'

The tall good-looking man she loved answered politely.

'Oh, just business. I'm on my way to the bank.' His brows were drawn in a straight line.

He clearly wasn't in an agreeable mood; she could tell that by just looking at him, and she was puzzled. The last time she'd seen him was the day they went to the cinema, and he'd been in a kissing mood then. The memory of that kiss returned as she viewed his firm, sensual lips. Sara wondered why he seemed bitter today. Had she done something wrong? What? Or perhaps he had business problems for the bank manager to solve. She decided not to poke or prod. She was uncertain of where she stood with him anyway. Looking back at their evening out, that kiss meant everything to her, but it may not have meant anything to him. Something cautioned her not to ask for explanations. She cleared her throat.

'You're on your way in and I'm on the way out. They'll be wondering where I am. I've been away too long already. See you!' He stood there, devilishly tempting, but she stepped to the side, intending to move on.

To her surprise, the curt tone of his voice brought her to an abrupt halt when he queried.

'Did you enjoy your tête-à-tête with Ken?'

'Pardon?' Looking up at his blue eyes and losing herself in their depths, she blinked and stared at him in astonishment.

She couldn't help notice the sarcastic nuances in his voice.

'You heard! I'm referring to your visit to Ken's bookshop a few minutes ago. I passed you in the street as you were about to go in.' There was almost a thread of warning in his voice. 'You waved at me, remember?'

The remark and his manner grated

on her nerves, and her hackles began to rise.

'Yes, I saw you. And?' She stared at him, slightly baffled.

'I expect you enjoyed the renowned Ken Fellow's personal attention?'

It was always hard to remain calm when she was close to him, but his approach irritated her because it was attacking and questioning.

'He saw me passing and invited me in. Is there anything wrong with that?'

A short silence was tight with tension. He didn't comment.

Sara's mouth had a resolute set, but she went on.

'He was being friendly.'

James chuckled nastily.

'Yes, Ken can be extremely affable when he chooses!'

Sara's temper didn't explode and then vanish. She'd learned to stand back and sometimes use her anger to her own advantage. She shook her head vigorously.

'I don't know what's got into you,

but this is a pretty stupid conversation. For some reason I don't understand, it seems that a perfectly innocent situation is worrying you. What's bothering you exactly?'

His lips were set in a determined line, and the skin was stretched tight across his cheekbones.

'He's out hunting and you're his current quarry.'

Her expression was thunderous and her face paled with anger. She held up her hand to silence him.

'Hold it! Ken is easy-going, and he's easy to get on with — and that's something I can't always say about you! I don't take him seriously, and I don't misconstrue his motives either.'

'Huh! Don't you? Then you should! You can't trust him further than you can throw him!' He leaned towards her and she could feel his breath on her face.

'What's got into you, James? I don't think you can be objective about Ken any more. You expect that he'll always be unprincipled, and you condemn him off-hand without giving him the slightest benefit of the doubt.'

'It seems he's found himself another champion!' James countered icily.

She paused and they eyed each other carefully. She tried to force her confused emotions into order and regain a sense of reality.

'Don't be silly! I'm trying to be fair, and act like an adult.' Her breath burned in her throat. 'Look, James — I know about what happened between Ken and you years ago. I can understand that you don't like him, but you were kids, and it was a long time ago. He was very stupid and it was very wrong of him, but why let it influence you for the rest of your life, especially as you two meet up all the time. You don't need to be friends, but you don't have to be suspicious about everything he says or does. I bet he regrets what happened more than anyone knows. I gather that it cost him a lot of friendships, not just yours. Why don't you just accept him as he is, try to ignore the past as much as you possibly can? Ken and I had a cup of coffee just now, and a chat; that's all. He was friendly and pleasant; as he has been whenever we've met.' Sara wondered why she was explaining or trying to arbitrate. 'Anyway, what I do, or don't do, is none of your business, is it? I'm no one's special friend, and no one's property.'

He inhaled sharply and gathered her into his arms.

The move was so unexpected her heartbeat skyrocketed as her soft curves moulded to the contours of his body. He pressed his lips to hers and she felt her knees weaken and her emotions whirl and skid. Raising his mouth from hers, their eyes locked and their breathing came in fast unison. He kissed her once again, more hungrily this time, and she stumbled backwards as she escaped the circle of his arms. Her lips were still warm from his kisses and she wished she could go on and enjoy the fiery sensations.

He gazed at her, and she could tell from the confusion in his eyes that he was organizing his thoughts, too. He managed to explain without sounding muddled or confused.

'I couldn't care less how he lives or what he does, but I don't want him to hurt you. I know him; and he's capable of doing just that!'

She ran her tongue over her lips and her hand through her hair. Her breathing was uneven.

'You're being over-melodramatic! We've met a couple of times, and had quite every-day conversations. He's never made a suggestive proposal or got too personal. He's never even invited me to the cinema or anywhere else!' Sara ignored his invitation to view his flat. 'Even if he had, may I remind you that it's my business what I do, and not yours! It's also his own business if he has affairs with women or not! I bet none of the women he's known were forced into an affair with him! He may act like a kind of man who thinks he'll get what he wants by sheer charm, but he's probably only successful because he chooses women who fall for it.' She looked at him defiantly. 'You can be certain I'm old enough to look after myself.'

He shrugged his shoulders and spread his hands.

'I wonder — are you?'

Sara was losing patience; she bit her lip and frowned. Who did he think he was to tell her what she should do? Even if her insides were still in turmoil, and she loved him, there was no reason he should try to dictate how she should think.

'This is ridiculous. I refuse to defend myself just because you've picked up some wrong impressions. I'm going home.' She moved away, her jaw tightening.

He halted her escape for a moment by placing his hand on her arm. He had scruples enough to sound apologetic.

'I'm sorry! You're right, of course. It's

none of my business. I didn't want you to get the wrong impression about Ken, that's all. You're new to the area and could easily be taken in by him.'

The annoyance receded and she looked up at him.

'I won't get any wrong ideas. If he's as experienced in handling women, as you say he is, he'll never try it on with me. Ken wants adulation and I can see that he's probably a practiced flirt, but he's not the only flirt I've met. I won't take him seriously, so don't give it a second thought.'

He smiled hesitatingly again.

'That's good!' He ran a finger down the curve of her cheek.

Sara had to struggle not to flinch. She longed to grab his hand and kiss him, but she resisted and gave him a weak smile instead. She was so confused that she didn't manage to ask him the most logical question of all — why he thought that his kisses and attention were acceptable, and any attention she got from Ken should be unacceptable.

Sara had never liked double standards in her business or private life, but she was discovering fast that she was prepared to make exceptions for someone she loved. She loved him too much to have enough courage to confront him and solicit an honest answer.

The tension lessened. He studied her for a moment before he stood aside with a sweeping gesture.

'Madam!'

She was glad to retort and welcome the lessening tension.

'Thank you, kind sir!' She moved past him. She looked back when she was inserting her key in the lock of her car door; he was still standing in the archway. He lifted his hand, before he strode away and was lost to sight.

8

Sara tried not to dwell on thoughts of James all the time, but it wasn't easy. He didn't seem to be the kind of man who sprinted from one relationship to the next, but he was young, single, good-looking, and very likeable in his serious way — all attractive attributes in the eyes of prospective girlfriends. What was there to stop him using them? She believed that he liked her — but how much? Was it just friendship, a passing fancy? He'd warned her about Ken purely out of personal antagonism and emotional tension could have triggered off his kissing her as he did. She couldn't decide if he was playing with her or not.

She tried to avoid phoning him, but in the end, she had to. The glasshouse lettuce was coming to an end and there'd be a gap until the next batch was ready. Half-way through dialling his number, she hesitated, but it was a business call and James was someone who appreciated the rules of commerce. As she listened to the phone ringing, she cleared her throat.

'James Conrad's office! Pamela Baker speaking. Can I help you?'

'Oh, Pamela!' Sara hurried to find the right words. 'Is James there? I'd like to speak to him, please.' Sara expected Pamela to say she'd pass the message on, but today must be one of her better days.

'Just a minute!' Pamela put the phone down and Sara heard her footsteps fading. In the distance, she heard Pamela shouting.

'James! James, darling! Sara's on the phone; she wants to speak to you.' Sara didn't try to catch the answer; she was too dazed. Pamela was calling him 'darling'? Was she his darling?

The unanswered question hammered her brain. She wanted to ignore it, but bitter thoughts emerged. Pamela was back again.

'Sorry Sara! He's very busy at present. Can I take a message?'

Pulling herself together, and with a steadiness in her voice that she didn't feel, she explained the reason for her call.

'I'll tell him,' Pamela replied. 'I've written it down, so you can be sure he'll get it. Thanks for letting us know. 'Bye!'

There was a click and the connection was cut. Sara sat with the phone hanging idly from her hand. Feeling rather shell-shocked, she was more doubtful than ever about James Conrad. Seconds later, her thoughts were also tinged with anger. He'd tried to blacken Ken in her eyes — but it was a case of the pot calling the kettle black? He was playing with her emotions and seemed to be involved with Pamela, too! Her thoughts swirled in a tangled web as she tried to think of a logical explanation.

Later that day, a phone call from

Aunt Margaret had never been more welcome; it diverted her thoughts. After a few preliminary enquiries about how things were, she utterly surprised Sara with a wonderful offer.

'Look Sara, I'm giving serious thought to moving permanently to Canada to be near Gaynor and her family. I'd like you to take over the garden permanently. It's running well, and I wouldn't be letting the workers down if you took over. I can't afford to give it to you as an outright gift, but I'll only want a fair price, so that I can live comfortably in Canada. I'll spread the cost over a long period for you, so that you don't need to burden yourself with a big bank loan — or you can sort another method out with the bank if you like. If you're interested, we can sort out the details later. If you don't want to take over, I'll probably just sell the whole lot off to the highest bidder.'

There was a moment of silence, as the significance sunk in. It was a wonderful offer, and Sara realized she'd like to accept. It was a lot of responsibility, and it was interesting work. She'd learned a lot about the business, and she had a ready-made team of good workers. The market garden was making a small, but steady profit.

'You've taken the wind out of my sails, and I know that it is a fantastic offer. I have to think about it seriously.'

'You do that! Talk about it to your parents, they're sensible people. It's a big decision, but somehow I think it would be right for you. I've just booked my flight, and I want to give you the details of that.'

With her thoughts still whirling, she said.

'Right! How are Gaynor and the twins? Is their brother coping okay?'

On to her favourite subject, her aunt sallied forth on descriptions of babies and her grandson. In the end, Sara had to remind her to give her the details, so that she'd be there to pick her up from the airport when she arrived.

* * *

She hadn't intended to go home for Easter, but unknowingly James was the reason she did. The day after her phone call about the glasshouse lettuce, he phoned back.

'Sorry I missed your call yesterday! I haven't had a chance to call till now.'

Sara swallowed the lump in her throat. 'Did Pamela pass on my message?'

'Yes. I'll find another source for a week until you have some more.'

Trying to keep the conversation rational, she replied, 'The new batch is coming on fine, but Bert says it needs another week or ten days to have real taste and enough body.'

'Good! But that isn't really my reason for calling.'

She waited.

'I'm going over to Brittany for the bank holiday. I wondered if you'd like to come?'

She fought for breath and her mind spun.

'Me?' She quickly searched her brain for a way out. She couldn't accept. She wanted commitment and she didn't know where she stood with him. Even though she loved him, a weekend affair was not for her — especially when his relationship with Pamela hung over her like a black cloud. Agitated and confused, she grabbed the first excuse that came to mind. 'I'm going home for Easter!'

'Oh!' He sounded genuinely disappointed. 'Couldn't you put it off?'

'No. My brother and his family are visiting, especially because I said I'll be coming home, too.'

Sara hoped the angels wouldn't punish her too much for lying.

There was a short silence.

'I should have asked you earlier; before you made plans. Pity! I suppose I'll go anyway and finish off the second bedroom.'

She bit her lip in dismay, glad that he couldn't see she was trying to control her thoughts.

'Sounds like a sensible idea,' she said, trying to control the faint thread of hysteria in her voice, and keep the conversation on rational ground. 'Sounds like you hoped to occupy me with a paintbrush for a couple of days!'

'I would have put you onto sanding and waxing the floor, actually!'

'Serves you right, then! Fancy inviting someone for the weekend, and then putting them to work!'

'If you'd come, I'd have enjoyed doing nothing for a couple of days! I promise you, we wouldn't have worked. Pleasure all the way!'

She struggled with her conscience for a couple of seconds, thought about Pamela, and decided she'd done the right thing. Sara forced lightness into her voice.

'Hope you enjoy yourself, and don't spend all the time working!'

'May as well get something finished. The rooms are very small. After I've sanded and waxed the floors and done the preparation work, I'll have to wait for things to settle before I can paint the walls, so I'm sure I'll have plenty of time to enjoy the local cooking and go for the occasional walk. Perhaps you'll give a thought to me covered in dust, and up to my eyes in paint. I'll think of you lazing with your family.'

The breath caught in her throat and her heart was heavy as lead as she thought about what it would have been like to be alone with him in a small two-bedroom cottage in a fishing village somewhere in Brittany.

'I have to go for now, Sara. Enjoy your weekend. I'll be seeing you!'

'You, too. 'Bye!' The connection was cut and Sara sat in lonely silence. She wondered if his next move would be to ask Pamela instead of her.

* * *

When Easter came, Sara tried not to feel regrets. She was doing the right thing. If her parents speculated about her sudden decision to come home again, or her preoccupied behaviour when she arrived, they didn't say so — they put it down to her aunt's offer. Sara hid her troubled thoughts by keeping her small nieces occupied with games, visits to the local playground, and taking them to see a Disney film. She saw the TV weather forecast, and that Brittany's was comparable. She wondered what the one person who meant everything to her was doing at that very moment.

Sara knew she had to make a decision about the market garden. Her parents thought it was a great idea, but it wasn't as easy as it seemed to them. The work, the financial aspects, the responsibility didn't bother her, but the uncertainty of knowing that she might have to live near James for the rest of her life was a prospect that circled her brain in never-ending circles. He might end up married to someone else; that would be hard to bear.

She didn't see, or hear, from him after the Bank Holiday weekend, and she made no move to get in touch. He was busy catching up on work, and Sara was torn two ways. She longed to see him, but didn't want to face him. A day or two later she met Pamela in the village. Sara was on her way to pick up some éclairs; they always helped when there was some serious thinking to be done. Somehow, she couldn't imagine Pamela doing her shopping at Ken's mother's shop, or that she was simply strolling along the roads for enjoyment. Sara studied her as she approached. She had an exaggerated sway that was meant to be sexy, but looked out of place on a village street. Pamela had never shown very much interest or friendliness, so Sara felt no necessity to stop for polite conversation. She'd almost passed her, when Pamela's voice stopped her in her tracks.

'Morning, Sara!' Her voice was perky and she looked pleased with herself.

'Morning!' Sara hesitated. 'It's unusual to see you in the village.'

Pamela gave a tinkling laugh.

'Yes, I suppose it is! But James's parents live here, so it's unavoidable. We're visiting them at the moment, but I forgot the bottle of wine James wanted to contribute to dinner, so I'm on my way to see if the local pub has anything worth drinking.' She looked around. 'Granted, it's not really my scene, but it is rustically pleasant. You seem to like it, and the people hereabouts, otherwise you wouldn't have taken part in the silliness of the pancake race.'

Sara straightened imperceptibly, and she tried not to feel annoyed.

'Yes, I like it because everyone knows one another and life moves at a slower pace. An awful lot of townies live out their lives in anonymous isolation. People care about each other here.'

'If you like that sort of thing!' Pamela shrugged and looked about vaguely. 'I suppose I'll have to accept being part of it all.'

Sara wondered where the conversation was heading. Was James moving his head office into one of the empty shops?

'And now that our professional relationship is a private one,' Pamela continued. 'I'll have to show interest whether I like it or not. His wife will have to, for his sake, if nothing else . . .'

With a touch of malicious concentration, Pamela saw how Sara's face collapsed with shocked surprise as the words sunk in. Sara's colour faded to a sickly hue.

'You and James? You're . . . ?' She felt ice spreading through her stomach.

Pamela lifted perfectly manicured, red-tipped fingers to give them a swift examination.

'Yes, but please don't tell anyone else yet. It's not general knowledge.' She tossed the mass of blonde hair over her shoulder and continued.

'I don't care a fig about official traditions, but James wants to go down the traditional path before making it public.'

Sara swallowed the despair in her throat and the pain in her heart. She stared, tongue-tied, and there was a sick and fiery gnawing somewhere inside. Her fears hadn't been ungrounded after all — she hadn't completely misjudged the risks of showing she loved him. She'd thought he wasn't a charlatan, but he'd kissed her while he was on the brink of getting engaged to Pamela. Why? Only because he noticed she was attracted to him and he'd felt sorry for her? She fought to keep any noticeable expression from her face, although the aching inside was growing by the minute and felt like an iron band tightening round her chest. Managing to surprise herself, the words came out calmly.

'Oh! Then I suppose congratulations are in order? I hope you'll both be very happy!' She was lying again, but didn't care if she had to pay off her dues in hell. Her only desire was to get away, and cope in secret with the harsh realities of misery.

Pamela beamed.

'Thank you! I'll pass your best wishes

on to James, of course.' She hesitated. 'I hear that you're on the brink of leaving soon?'

Stiffly Sara responded, her nails digging into her clenched hands.

'My aunt is due back next week. Once I've handed over the office, I'll be off.' After hearing Pamela's news, it couldn't come quick enough.

Pamela nodded.

'Then you probably won't see James again. He'll be visiting a couple of suppliers in Germany and he's likely to be gone for ten days.' She added in a confidential tone. 'I'm wondering if it wouldn't be a perfect chance for us to get away together. If I go, we could have a couple of evenings on the banks of the Rhine in one of those cosy wine-cellars.' She laughed softly.

Sara was silent and her throat was raw with unuttered shouts and protests. She had to hide her true feelings.

'Have a nice time if you go. 'Bye, Pamela!' Sara turned and walked away swiftly. She swallowed hard and bit back tears. She was glad not to meet anyone she knew on her way back to the car. When she was inside, tears slowly found their way down her cheeks. Brushing them away with the back of her hand, she drove home feeling so upset that she couldn't even remember why she had gone to the village in the first place.

9

In the early hours of the morning, Sara got up and went to the bedroom window where she looked out unseeingly over the garden. It was a still dawn, cold and misty. She felt drained, hollow and lifeless; felt like crying, was vulnerable and very alone. Although she'd found the one person she'd wanted for the rest of her life, the ground beneath her feet had opened up. She had to accept that James belonged to someone else. She'd woken up from a restless sleep; from vestiges of broken dreams that she was trying to hang on to someone or something that drew further and further away despite all her efforts. Sara realized she still hadn't come to terms with the situation — but she was determined she would! She threw back her shoulders and went to sit on the wide windowsill, hugging her knees and ignoring the goosepimples. Life went on, and she'd get through the misery somehow. She had her work and her family and friends. She had nothing to reproach herself with, even though she felt an acute sense of loss.

The most important thing she had to settle was whether to accept Aunt Margaret's offer or not. She'd be back in a couple of days. Her crushed emotions told her she couldn't stay in the village; common sense told her she'd be stupid to turn down such a generous offer. Could she take over the market garden knowing James was living not very far away with someone else? He was only one of many customers; they could exist without him. It was a feasible possibility to gradually persuade him to go elsewhere, by continually quoting prices beyond his budget. Would that work?

The arguments for, and against, continued to run along well-worn grooves in her brain.

That afternoon, she came back from delivering vegetables to find some messages on the answering machine. One was from James, asking her to phone him before he left for Germany that evening. She ignored it and took the phone off the hook. Having to talk to him at the moment was something she couldn't cope with, she'd have to congratulate him and listen to things she didn't want to hear.

* * *

The supermarket was busy. Sara almost walked passed Annie Conrad without noticing her.

'Hello, Sara!'

Sara stopped in her tracks and returned the greeting.

'Here selling vegetables to the enemy?' she enquired jokingly.

Sara shook her head.

'We're too pricey for them. I wanted fish for supper and this is the only place I know where you can get fresh fish.'

'That's true. I try to do all my shopping in the village, but Martha doesn't stock everything, so I come in once a month to get the things she doesn't have.' She looked around briefly. 'Are you in an awful hurry? Have you time for a cup of coffee before you leave?'

Sara was confused by the unexpected invitation, but she nodded.

'Yes.' She pointed towards the rows of shelves. 'I'll just finish my shopping. Perhaps we can meet in the bistro next to the entrance — in about ten or fifteen minutes?'

'Lovely!' Mrs Conrad gave her a searching look. The younger woman looked pale, and her normally bright eyes lacked any lustre. Her face was thin and strained. 'See you in a couple of minutes, then!'

They went in opposite directions to disappear among the maze of shelves.

A short time later, Sara was facing James's mother across the bistro table, she fingered the large cup of frothy cappuccino and eyed her expectantly.

'You and James are good friends aren't you?' Mrs Conrad said.

Sara swallowed the lump in her throat.

'Yes, I think so; considering that we haven't known each other very long.'

'You'll be leaving, when Maggie returns? I'll be very sorry to see you go and I'm sure James will, too.' She reached out and touched Sara's hand briefly. 'I like you, Sara, otherwise I wouldn't have got up the courage to talk to you like this. Some instinct tells me you like James a lot, and I'm positive he feels the same about you. Please sort things out before you go. He's like a bear with a sore head at the moment!'

Sara wet her lips. She didn't want to comment, or give herself away. Her brown eyes met Mrs Conrad's blue ones and they stared silently at each other. With her eyes glistening, Sara managed to reply.

'Mrs Conrad, I don't think we should

be discussing James like this; he and I are friends, nothing more.'

The older woman waved her hands around nervously.

'I know that and I know that I shouldn't interfere, James would probably kill me with his bare hands if he knew . . . '

Somewhere deep inside Annie Conrad's interest was reviving some of her hopes, but then Sara remembered her meeting with Pamela. Mothers often completely miscalculated their children, however well they thought they knew them. Sara drew a deep breath.

'I think you're mixing things up. Pamela told me the other day that she and James were practically on the brink of getting engaged.'

Mrs Conrad's expression was pure shock and her eyebrows lifted.

'James and Pamela? Rubbish! James would have given us some kind of indication long ago. He wouldn't spring something like that on us. I don't believe it for a second!' She looked reflective for a few seconds. 'Know what? She's trying to frighten you off!'

Sara stared slightly baffled.

'If he hasn't told you yet, he may be going to, soon.'

Mrs Conrad shook her head.

'No! Pamela may be an excellent assistant, but she can't make him fall in love with her — however much she'd like that to happen.'

'But she wouldn't tell a blatant lie; if someone found out she was lying about something like that, she'd look very stupid wouldn't she?'

'She's not stupid; she's clever and manipulative! She wouldn't dare spread a rumour like that around publicly. I bet she hasn't told anyone else, and she's reckoning with the fact you won't either, and will leave without seeing James again!'

Sara's thoughts were whirling.

'I know that she unexpectedly organized some appointments abroad for James. I bet she reckons that you'll be gone before he gets back.' She leaned forward slightly. 'But I happen to know James is coming back specially to see you before you leave. So please don't go before he gets here! You can't imagine how often your name creeps into his conversation these days; even his dad remarked about it the other day. That alone speaks volumes. We've never seen him react about a girl like this before.'

The colour was gradually deepening on Sara's cheeks.

'I'm not going to chase him or wear my heart on my sleeve!'

Mrs Conrad sighed in exasperation.

'Heavens! With your attitude and my son's approach, there's a danger that you'll never sort things out.' The older woman smiled and sighed softly. 'Take my advice and show him you want more than friendship — I think he feels the same way about you. You have nothing to lose! He's coming back earlier than Pamela expects — tomorrow, in fact.'

Wordlessly, Sara nodded, and a growing sense of breathless agitation was unfolding inside. Perhaps his mother was right. Perhaps there was an explanation and she still had a chance. He at least deserved a chance to explain, and it would be better to hear the truth from his own lips . . .

10

It took him barely 15 minutes to arrive at the door. He'd stopped on the way at Fred's Bakery and picked up some fresh éclairs. He didn't know what it was all about, but he didn't care; she'd phoned him and asked him to come, and that was more than enough for him.

Even though it was mid-morning and she knew that he was busy, Sara felt no guilt. Since she'd talked to his mother, she'd thought and thought about the craziest way to get him here and keep him long enough to tell him she loved him. She had to fight if she wanted him, and she was now determined to show him just how much. She met him at the door, wrapped in nothing but her pink dressing gown and his big, blue eyes were wide with surprise. There was a tingling in the pit of her stomach.

Handing her the box with the éclairs silently, his eyes raked boldly over her.

'Do you know what time it is? he asked. 'Have you been drinking?'

The smouldering flame she saw in his eyes excited her. His mother was right. With a flush on her cheeks, she took the box from him.

'How scrumptious! Thanks!' She placed it on the kitchen table and turned back to him. She'd found a bottle of Piper-Heidsieck in Aunt Margaret's fridge last night, and it was beautifully cold and perfect for drinking. 'No, I haven't been drinking, but I hope that we're about to, together.' She hurried to hand him the champagne.

At the sight of the outstretched bottle of champagne, he shook his head, but accepted it, removed the foil covering and expertly popped the cork. He still wondered why she'd told him to come. She made a mad and completely alluring picture and she took his breath away; it was an effort to concentrate on opening the bottle. It made a satisfying popping sound.

'Do you mind telling me what this is all about? What's so special that it can't wait?' He smiled back at her as he adjusted to the situation, and she had the feeling he was beginning to get into the swing of things at last. He poured some of the pale yellow liquid into the two long-stemmed glasses and the bubbles began to rise. He put the bottle down, picked up the glasses and held one of them out towards her. 'Is it your birthday?'

She took it, shook her head vigorously. 'I'd never dress like this for any customer, except you — in fact I've never done anything like this before! And it isn't my birthday either!'

His eyes began to twinkle. 'Then I can only presume it's my birthday.'

She was desperate to break down any barriers between them without complicated explanations, not yet. Explanations took too long; she wanted his arms around her. 'Don't ask why

I'm acting like a loony, James.' She put her finger to his lips. 'Just tell me that you like me a lot; I'm hoping that you'll say you love me a little!'

He was at a loss for a moment, and looked slightly stunned, but then he promptly admitted without any effort.

'Yes, yes! As a matter of fact, I do love you. I love you more than I thought it was possible to love anyone. I've been trying to get you in the right mood to tell you so for some time now, but you kept twisting and turning like an eel in a muddy pool without sufficient water. Recently I began to wonder if you just didn't want to know. The last couple of days have been agony, because I couldn't figure out what you felt.'

Her heartbeat rocketed.

'I know. It may have looked like I was dodging you, but it was only because I didn't know if you were serious or not. I'm hoping you'll tell me there is no reason for me to doubt you; that you love me and won't change your mind.'

'I don't know what's got into you,' he said huskily. 'But I'll go along with all of this, because it gives me the chance I've waited for. Of course I love you. I love you like crazy! I always will. You know me well-enough to know that I keep my word. I won't change my mind; I'll never change my mind about loving you.'

'I'm sorry I was such an idiot,' she said, looking up. 'I imagined all the wrong things; picked up all the wrong signals. I tried to ignore you and push you away because I thought you were in love with Pamela — especially after she told me you two were on the brink of getting engaged . . . '

He looked shell-shocked and then outraged.

'In love with Pamela? Engaged? Me?' His voice had gone up an octave. He ran his fingers through his hair and the expression of disbelief in his eyes deepened. 'She told you that, and you believed her?' Sara saw he was trying to keep his growing anger under control.

'Just wait until I get back to the office; she'll be looking for a new job tomorrow morning! How could you believe her, why didn't you get in touch — ask me, or even ask my mother?' He put the glass down and took her into his arms.

Sara looked up into his eyes and snuggled closer. It was heaven.

'It was your mother who told me she thought our wires were tangled, and then I came to my senses and began to hope. She said we ought to sort things out before it was too late. Your mother realises I'm in love with you, that's why she encouraged me to get in touch.' He stiffened slightly and Sara tried to take the fat out of the fire. 'She cares — otherwise she wouldn't have said anything.'

'Tell me something — has the world gone completely mad? I was determined to see you today anyway — I had no intention of letting you go without trying to find out how we really felt about each other.' He paused for a second as her words sunk in. 'I can't believe you thought that I liked Pamela in that kind of way. She's an excellent assistant, but that's all. Not my type at all — you are, my love! When I met you I knew you were the 'One' from the word go. I tried to build up trust, was jealous of Ken, and we clashed. Surely you guessed I was attracted? Do the men you know go around kissing women at random? I assure you, I don't. I'm serious about you, otherwise I wouldn't have wanted to kiss you.' His voice drifted into a hushed whisper. 'The only thing I want in the world is for you to love me, and it seems that you do! If this is a dream, I don't ever want to wake up.' Seeing the expression on her face, he enclosed her more tightly in his arms. 'I thought time was running out for us, but now we're beginning to sort things out at last. We'll have to figure out how we can see one another regularly if you have to work elsewhere, or perhaps you can find a permanent job locally. That would be a really good solution.'

'We don't really know one another properly yet, do we? But we will have lots of time — all the time in the world.' Sara told him about her aunt's offer.

He gave a whoop, and his eyes shone fiercely.

She brought her glass of champagne awkwardly up between their lips and they both took a sip. Sara handed him the glass. It gave her enough elbow room and time to begin to unfasten the buttons of his shirt. His eyebrows lifted.

'And this is how you propose we talk things through?' He studied her with loving affection, and he chuckled. 'Remind me to send my mother a huge bunch of flowers when we come down to earth again!'

She started to laugh and he joined in; the sound echoed through the room. They grew silent and viewed each other with knowing eyes. They kissed, safe in the knowledge of belonging. At last Sara could see how his eyes were full of fun and laughter. They glowed with an inner fire, and she kissed him. She was aware of every movement, of every sensation, and knew he was feeling exactly the same. She felt happier than she'd ever felt in her life before, and knew they were going to be all right. He grinned and straightened his shoulders. She knew him in a way no one else did, or ever would. He'd let her into his world with no barricade or restrictions and explanations were unnecessary. She was sure any explanations could wait until much, much later; now they had better things to do . . .

THE END

We do hope that you have enjoyed reading this large print book.

Did you know that all of our titles are available for purchase?

We publish a wide range of high quality large print books including:
Romances, Mysteries, Classics
General Fiction
Non Fiction and Westerns

Special interest titles available in large print are:
The Little Oxford Dictionary
Music Book, Song Book
Hymn Book, Service Book

Also available from us courtesy of Oxford University Press:
Young Readers' Dictionary
(large print edition)
Young Readers' Thesaurus
(large print edition)

For further information or a free brochure, please contact us at:

Other titles in the Linford Romance Library:

CHRISTMAS AT HARTFORD HALL

Fenella Miller

When Elizabeth's grandfather died, there was no sign of a will; and, devastatingly, she discovered she was now dependent on his heir. When the new Lord and Lady Hartford and their twin daughters arrived, they reduced her status to that of a servant. Elizabeth is determined to leave Hartford Hall in the New Year and find work as a governess. But the arrival of Sir James Worthington to make an offer for Lady Eleanor only adds to her difficulties . . .

ABIGAIL MOOR: THE DARKEST DAWN

Valerie Holmes

Miss Abigail Hammond grows up in Beckton Manor as the adopted daughter of Lord Hammond. However, when he falls terminally ill, her life, her identity and her safety are all threatened. Then, faced with being forced into a marriage to a man she loathes, she runs away with her maid on Lord Hammond's instructions. Abigail tries to discover the truth of her past, despite her efforts being constantly foiled by her life-long maid, Martha.

STRANGERS IN THE NIGHT

Beth James

The man of her dreams sweeps Dee into a romantic last dance at her friend's wedding — then promptly disappears. When they meet again, it's in unpleasant circumstances. She finds that they are on opposite sides in a conflict that involves a promise Dee made to her favourite aunt. There is no way to resolve the situation — Dee cannot compromise, yet her heart tells her that Jack is the man for her. Sometimes however, love will find a way . . .

OLD DESIRES

Liz Fielding

Joshua Kent infuriated Holly — he was arrogant, overbearing and convinced she was a good-for-nothing gold-digger! But even worse was his bombshell that her past was a complete fabrication. A new identity — and the inheritance which went with it — meant that Holly could embark on a fresh life for herself. But where did Joshua fit into the scheme of things? Was he just using the desire which flared between them to manipulate her? Only time would tell . . .

OUT OF THE BLUE

Chrissie Loveday

Bryher is tempted into a race on her motorbike one morning, with little idea of the chain of events that will follow. A new job leads to an unexpected meeting and a whole new career. Tristan seems to think an attractive female can oil the wheels of business. Never! She might fall for another biker, or a surfer perhaps . . . but an accountant? There's certainly no future here . . . or is there?

THE TURN OF THE TIDE

Penelope Alexander

In the North Cornish village of Penarren, widow Jenny Hawke and her family struggle to keep The Chough café going. When Kit Venning returns, causing controversy, Jenny, unexpectedly, falls in love with him. Then Kit joins the crew of the lifeboat *Etta Trelawney*. It takes dramatic events at sea and the rescue of Jenny's grandson, Ben, to settle past difficulties between the Trelawneys and Vennings . . . and to help Jenny and Kit realise what they mean to each other.